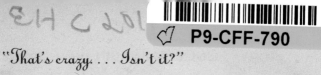

"That's crazy. . . . Isn't it?"

"You've said yourself Mr. Hartley has threatened to shut us down. Word can get out pretty quickly. Maybe he's here scouting."

"Like a spy?"

Beth shrugged. "It could happen."

What if Will had been snooping in the kitchen? Maybe he was planning to turn the camp into a resort. The room with the Ping-Pong table would be turned into a spa and the cafeteria into a restaurant with white tablecloths and votives on tiny tables.

Cassie chased the thoughts out of her mind. "Will seems pretty harmless."

Beth looked behind her and then leaned in close again. "I've heard his father has had his eye on this camp for years, ever since he made so much money on the campgrounds south of town. He had meetings at the church headquarters in Oklahoma City, but they turned him down."

Cassie shielded her eyes from the sun.

"Be careful around him," Beth said. "His family is powerful."

JULIE JARNAGIN grew up in a rural community where her family farmed and raised cattle, inspiring her to set much of her fiction in small towns. She earned a BA in journalism/professional writing from the University of Oklahoma and is a member of American Christian Fiction Writers. Her articles have appeared in local and national publications. Through her writing, she hopes to share stories that reflect God's love.

Julie lives in Oklahoma with her husband and young son. Visit her website at www.JulieJarnagin.com.

Canyon Walls

Julie Jarnagin

Heartsong Presents

To my husband, Kevin. Your love and support mean the world to me. I love you today, tomorrow, and always.

A note from the Author:
I love to hear from my readers! You may correspond with me by writing:

Julie Jarnagin
Author Relations
PO Box 721
Uhrichsville, OH 44683

ISBN 978-1-61626-332-4

CANYON WALLS

Scripture taken from the HOLY BIBLE, NEW INTERNATIONAL VERSION®. NIV®. Copyright © 1973, 1978, 1984, 2010 by Biblica, Inc.™ Used by permission. All rights reserved worldwide.

Our mission is to publish and distribute inspirational products offering exceptional value and biblical encouragement to the masses.

PRINTED IN THE U.S.A.

one

The metal shelf creaked as Cassie Langley teetered on the edge, stretching her fingers to the toolbox just out of reach.

"Let me help you with that."

Cassie flinched and almost lost her balance. She hadn't heard the man walk into the cafeteria pantry. She wrapped her fingers around a wooden broom handle beside her to regain her balance. "No thank you," she said without turning to see his face. "I can reach it myself."

She had managed to run the church camp for the last nine months, supervising the staff, taking care of the grounds, and working with the kids. She didn't need help with a simple task like reaching a toolbox.

She pushed a box of napkins out of her way and waited to hear him leave, but the room was silent except for the rumble of the walk-in freezer. "Is there something I can help you with? Are you lost?"

His footsteps moved closer. "Just looking for a piece of rope."

She stood on one foot, letting the other lift up behind her as she reached farther for the toolbox. "Rope?"

"I'm a counselor this week. One of the boys in my cabin is trying to play tag football, but his baggy pants keep tripping him up. He needs a belt."

Her fingers touched the plastic handle. "Got it!" As she pulled the toolbox closer to her, her foot slipped. She reached for the broom handle to keep from falling to the concrete floor.

5

His hand cupped her elbow and supported her. "Whoa, are you sure you won't let me help you?"

Cassie was losing her patience with this guy. She steadied herself on the shelf. "No thank you. I'm fine."

She didn't need help, especially from a volunteer who would be gone at the end of the week. Of course, it wasn't this stranger's fault that she was having a tough day.

She took a deep breath. "The rope is in the top drawer by the kitchen sink. Help yourself."

When he didn't move, she sighed loud enough for him to hear. "I'm fine," she said. "I've got it. Really."

As she stepped back off the shelf and pulled the toolbox with her, she felt something snap. Hammers, screwdrivers, pliers, and nails poured out of the box above her head. She yelled and shielded her eyes. Something heavy, possibly a wrench, slammed against her shoulder, narrowly missing her head.

She fell backward, but an arm wrapped around her middle, keeping her from hitting the floor below. A hand took the toolbox.

Her cheeks burned with anger at whoever had put the toolbox back without latching the lid and at the stranger who thought she needed saving.

"Are you okay?" he asked.

Cassie pulled away from him. She crouched to the floor and grabbed tools, throwing them back into the box. Her shoulder throbbed. "I'm fine. They're definitely going to hear about this at the staff meeting."

She looked up, seeing him for the first time as he bent down and reached for a nail that had rolled under a crate of apples. He was handsome—too handsome—with chiseled features and tan skin. Like he had walked straight out of a catalog. But she wasn't attracted to the kind of men with big egos and expectations that females would swoon over them.

She reminded herself that this man wasn't her father. She needed to be professional, despite her first impressions of him. "Come on. I'll show you where we keep the rope."

He let out a chuckle and then sucked air back through his mouth when she looked at him.

Her mouth fell open. "You're laughing at me?"

"No, I'm not laughing at you. I'm just. . ."

She put her hands on her hips as she stood. "Just what?"

"Well, okay, I'm laughing a little, but you're so mad. I tried to help you, but you wouldn't let me."

She glared at him. "I didn't need your help. I had reached it, but someone left it open."

He held his hands up in front of him. "I know. I know. I'm sorry."

She looked up at him. He was tall, almost a foot taller than her own five-foot-three-inch frame.

"I'm Will Overman. You must be Cassie." He stuck out his hand.

She slipped the screwdriver into her pocket and placed her palm on his. Will's hand covered hers. Their eyes met, but Cassie promised herself she wouldn't fall for his charm, which in her experience usually turned out to be arrogance. A well-worn University of Oklahoma T-shirt stretched across his torso. He had probably spent more time fixing his dark wavy hair than she had spent on her own. Handsome didn't mean much to Cassie.

"I've heard about you," he said, following her out of the pantry.

She walked faster. "Oh?" If he had heard of her, it could only mean he lived in Wyatt Bend. In a small town, people talked.

The camp was nestled in a canyon not far from Wyatt Bend, Oklahoma, and the people there had always claimed it as their own. They had opinions on everything that happened there, something Cassie still hadn't grown to accept. Growing up, she learned that the more she did on her own, the less she risked being let down by other people.

Beth, the camp cook, had already warned her that word of the changes at the camp had made its way around the local beauty salons and coffee shops.

"You took over after Henry Mason retired," Will said, as if he was telling her some piece of information never revealed to her. "Everybody loves Henry."

Henry Mason was a small-town hero, active in the largest church in town, and a member of the school board. What they didn't know was that Cassie was cleaning up everything he hadn't had time for, like keeping the camp afloat, maintaining books, and following all the required codes.

It wasn't that Henry was a bad man; he just didn't care about the details that came with the job. Budgets, bills, and paperwork had obviously fallen to the bottom of his priority list. Cassie had spent the last nine months trying to keep the church board from shutting down Sunset Camp. According to her boss, who spent his days in an office in Oklahoma City running several sites throughout the state, the camp was costing the conference more and more every year, and he struggled to justify the camp's financial losses at the board meetings.

Cassie couldn't imagine the camp closing, especially after it had touched so many lives, including her own.

Will followed her through the kitchen. "Do you ever hear from Henry?"

"Every now and then," Cassie said. "He likes Arizona."

Will leaned against the giant stainless-steel utility sink. "Good for him. We really miss him at church."

Cassie found the rope exactly where she had told him it

would be. She tossed it at him, and he caught it as it hit his chest. Pulling a screwdriver from the deep pocket of her cargo pants, she said, "I have to go. I need to open someone's suitcase."

"Hang on," Will said. "I have a question for you."

The glint in his eye told her he was teasing her. "Okay."

Mimicking her, he crossed his arms. "Why do you keep the toolbox on the top shelf of the pantry behind those huge boxes? Are you hiding something in there?"

She rolled her eyes. "If you must know, a few months ago a girl found a screwdriver in one of the drawers. After her counselors fell asleep, she removed the screen window by her bunk and snuck out to meet a boy."

"Wow. She went to a lot of work."

Cassie wiped a smudge off the oven with the hem of her shirt. "You have to give some of them points for creativity."

Will ducked under the pot rack that hung beside the giant gas stove. "Why didn't she go out the door?"

Obviously Will was an amateur when it came to the art of sneaking out of cabins. He was going to be in for a long week of volunteering. "Do you think we don't have a good reason for not greasing the squeaky hinges? Have you ever heard one of those doors open?"

The light from the windows reflected off a silver cross on the chain around his neck. He smiled a broad smile and pointed at her. "They don't know who they're up against, do they?"

"They don't know I was a camper once, too, and an expert at sneaking out to the bonfire site," she said, a little embarrassed to admit it to a stranger.

Eyes bright and wide, he nodded. "Ah, you probably blazed the trail for some of them. Do you have any tips for my survival this week?"

Before Cassie could answer, something outside the window caught her eye. Beth marched across the lawn toward the cafeteria. Her telltale crimson cheeks revealed something had her riled. "I have to go."

"What's wrong?"

Cassie's long ponytail swung as she spun around to the screen door. "It looks like I have work to do."

"Can I help?"

Cassie laughed as she walked outside. "No thank you."

Cassie sat beside Beth, who had collapsed on the wooden bench in front of the game hall.

"What's wrong? Is it one of the kids?" Cassie asked.

Beth shook her head. "No, nothing like that."

A weight lifted off Cassie's chest, knowing there wouldn't be a trip to the emergency room. "Well?"

"Only a canceled delivery, but without that food, I'll have to rearrange my entire menu."

A camp counselor wearing overalls and pigtails pulled the rope to ring the huge bell in the middle of the yard. Excited campers flooded the gravel road to the cabins, girls to the right, boys to the left.

"Plus, you won't believe who's here this week," she said.

Cassie used her unpolished nail to scrape off a heart drawn on the arm of the bench. "A bunch of teenagers who are going to be the death of me?"

Beth pushed a piece of short blond hair away from her eyes. "I'm serious."

Beth was a bit of a drama queen. The chaos usually involved a man, but Cassie loved her big heart. Cassie sat up and crossed her ankles. "I'm sorry. I'm listening. What's going on?"

"I was helping some counselors set up a check-in table, and I saw. . ." Will walked out of the kitchen.

Beth squeaked.

He waved at Cassie with a sly smile and turned to walk toward the boys' cabins.

"That's Will Overman. What's the problem?" The scenario formed in Cassie's mind. "Oh no. Do you have a crush on him? Did you date him? Did he dump you?"

"Would you stop and listen to me?" Beth said.

Cassie bit her bottom lip.

"He's Will Overman of Overman Real Estate."

Cassie stared at her, trying to understand. "And?"

"Do you ever read the local paper?"

The pace of life in a small town had been a culture shock when Cassie moved from Albuquerque. "Don't have time. Besides, it's all family reunions and updates on the crops."

"You need to listen to town gossip a little more." Beth leaned close to Cassie. "The Overmans are loaded. Will's dad, Leonard, and his sons are responsible for the tourism boom in town. They bought a bunch of property around the state park and built cabins for people coming from the city."

"That doesn't sound too bad. Don't we need to get started on dinner?"

Beth's chin dropped to her chest. "Will works for the family business. I can't believe he took off an entire week to come here. Maybe they're looking to buy more land. Maybe they heard someone was selling in the canyon."

"You think Will and his family want to buy our canyon?"

"Why not?" Beth asked.

"That's crazy. . . . Isn't it?"

"You've said yourself Mr. Hartley has threatened to shut us down. Word can get out pretty quickly. Maybe he's here scouting."

"Like a spy?"

Beth shrugged. "It could happen."

What if Will had been snooping in the kitchen? Maybe

he was planning to turn the camp into a resort. The room with the Ping-Pong table would be turned into a spa and the cafeteria into a restaurant with white tablecloths and votives on tiny tables.

Cassie chased the thoughts out of her mind. "Will seems pretty harmless."

Beth looked behind her and then leaned in close again. "I've heard his father has had his eye on this camp for years, ever since he made so much money on the campgrounds south of town. He had meetings at the church headquarters in Oklahoma City, but they turned him down."

Cassie shielded her eyes from the sun.

"Be careful around him," Beth said. "His family is powerful."

two

A wad of paper sailed across the room and landed between two girls in the front row. Will cringed and shot a stern look at the fourteen-year-old boy who now had his head bowed with the rest of the campers.

What was he doing here? Piles of work would be waiting for him next week. Letting the youth pastor talk him into spending a week at the camp had seemed like the right thing to do, but now he wasn't sure.

With the word "amen," Will looked to the small stage. He wasn't the only one giving a week of his time. The leaders, counselors, and musicians were all volunteering despite their busy lives.

Two boys from his cabin whispered as a pastor led the group in a devotional. Will cleared his throat and they quieted, slumping in their seats. It would take more than a few hours to reach them, and he was unsure if he could make any difference in a week.

Things had changed since he had been a camper here. The tabernacle had been nothing more than a concrete slab with wood poles holding up a metal roof. He remembered the time a diamondback rattlesnake interrupted the service. Today the building was enclosed, air-conditioned, and had a sound system and a projector for song lyrics. The rumor was that an anonymous donor, someone who had heard about the camp's financial struggles, had funded the improvements.

A man on a stool onstage played an electric guitar. Everyone stood. Will slipped out of his chair to stand at the back of the room where he could keep an eye on the boys.

Cassie sat in a chair against the wall with her eyes closed and her mouth slightly open. The need to take care of her rushed over him. The feeling caught him off guard as it had when he first saw her standing on the shelf in the cafeteria. She had made it clear she didn't want his help.

When the service ended and campers streamed out the doors, he sat beside her. "There are probably quieter places to take a nap."

Her eyes jolted open, and she ran her fingers across the bottom edge of her mouth. "I can't believe I fell asleep," she said, glancing side to side. "It's been a long week."

He leaned toward her. "It's only Monday."

She groaned. "Oh no. It *is* going to be a long week."

Will put his hands on the back of his head and leaned against the wall. He wouldn't mind a nap.

"But it's worth it," Cassie said.

He shifted in his seat. "It brings back a lot of memories for me. That's for sure."

She tilted her head. "What do you mean?"

"From when I was a camper."

Her face softened. "Here? When?"

"Let's see. . ." Will calculated the math in his head. "My first summer was about fifteen years ago, and I came every summer until high school."

"What made you stop coming?"

Will waved to one of the boys from his cabin who pulled the hood of his sweatshirt over his head. "Football camp."

"Ah."

"What about you?" he asked. "Were you a camper here?"

"Sounds like we were here the same summers," she said.

He studied her, sure he would have remembered her big brown eyes and wide smile.

"We probably never met. I was part of the camp for the intercity ministry," she said.

"Really?"

She stiffened. "You sound surprised."

"I just wouldn't have guessed."

She shrugged. "After my dad left, I spent my summers with my grandparents in Oklahoma City. Their church offered to pay so I could attend."

"Where did you grow up?"

"Albuquerque. My sister always stayed home. She couldn't stand to be away from our mom all summer."

Cassie must have been a brave girl, attending a camp where she didn't know anyone. Most of the campers from his church tended to flock together on the first day of camp. "This place probably felt like a different planet compared to a big city like Albuquerque."

"Camp was the best part of my year," she said so quietly he didn't know whether she meant for him to hear.

Will's gaze moved from a group of teenagers lingering in a corner to Cassie. "You really love it here. Don't you?"

"I do." She stared at him like she was sizing him up until he broke her gaze.

&

The next morning Cassie dragged herself into the kitchen to find Beth behind the giant griddle. The smell of sausage drifted through the room. "Good morning, sunshine," Beth, the epitome of a morning person, said.

Usually Cassie arrived to the cafeteria first, but she hadn't slept much that night. All the thoughts and worries she had tried to push out of her mind all day had rushed back. If Will was there to spy, should she confront him? Should she call her boss and see if anything was going on?

"I need coffee and lots of it," Cassie said. "Have you made

the real stuff yet?"

The "real" coffee was brewed in a small pot in Beth's tiny office. Beth ground the coffee beans she kept hidden in a drawer. The huge dispenser of coffee they served to exhausted counselors was less expensive and brewed by the gallon. They let only the most desperate volunteers in on their secret; otherwise it disappeared before Cassie got more than one mug.

"It's in there waiting for you. Rough night?"

It had been too hot for Cassie to sleep under the quilt on her bed. She had stared at the ceiling and resolved to keep a close eye on Will Overman during the week. Even if he wasn't there to take her camp out from under her, she didn't trust men like him. Will had probably never worried about money in his entire life and never stopped to realize the people around him might have had a very different life.

When Cassie came to Sunset Camp as a camper, she arrived as a broken kid, abandoned by her father. During her week at the camp, she learned she had another father, a heavenly Father. It had changed her life, and it still changed lives today.

"Did the missing delivery mess up your menu?" Cassie asked.

Beth poured perfect circles of batter on the griddle with one hand while flipping the pancakes on the back row with a spatula. "It worked out for the best. I switched to pancakes instead of the omelets. The blueberries will be fresher today anyway."

Cassie was blessed to have such a capable staff working with her. Emory, who was seventy-five years young, still drove down to the canyon several days a week to take care of mowing their grass and help with maintenance.

The morning sunlight streamed in from the tall windows

across the east walls. "I'd better get some work done before breakfast."

"I'll save you something to eat." A timer behind Beth dinged.

"What about you?" Cassie asked. "Are you having breakfast?"

Beth held up the spatula, batter dripping off the side. "Can't. I'm back on my diet."

This was her third diet in five weeks. Cassie didn't approve of Beth's crazy diets, but from the look on her face, now wasn't the right time to talk about it. Cassie mentally added it to her list of things to pray about.

Cassie left the kitchen and walked through the dining area. A narrow hallway led to a wing of the building that housed their camp offices. A glass door at the end of the hall opened to the outside. After pouring herself a mug of coffee in Beth's office, Cassie walked into her own small office. Paper, binders, and receipts were stacked in neat piles on every open surface, including the windowsill. Books sat in the two straight-backed chairs across from the desk. Beside the door was a basket of loose slips of paper. Cassie had spent months going through every bill, checkbook, or ledger she could find to organize all the camp's paperwork.

While the old computer sputtered, Cassie stared out the window at the creek running through the canyon. As she waited for her e-mail to open, she wrapped her hands around the mug and took a sip of her still-steaming coffee.

A dinging noise indicated she had new e-mails. As she scrolled through the list, she stopped when she saw Marvin Hartley's name. Her boss rarely sent her e-mails. Mr. Hartley was the director over all the denomination's camps in the state. He had once told her that e-mail was too impersonal; although one wouldn't say that Mr. Hartley was very personable face-to-face. At the time, she thought he didn't know how to use the fancy computer in his office, but when she received a handwritten note a few weeks later, she decided he was just old-fashioned.

Her foot bounced as she waited for the box to open.

> *Dear Miss Langley:*
> *I will be in the area next Monday, and I would like to sit down and discuss some of the issues of the camp. Please respond to let me know if this day will work with your schedule.*
>
> *Regards,*
> *Marvin Hartley*

Cassie reread the message three times. She repeated the words *the issues* over and over in her head.

She rarely saw her boss. He had news, and she prayed it would be good.

When her predecessor left the camp, Mr. Hartley had told Cassie her move from the job of assistant director to the position of director was temporary. Was her time as interim director coming to an end?

There was a knock on her door. Cassie minimized the message even though no one, except maybe Beth, would suspect the benign note could be a warning.

"Cassie, are you in here?"

Will.

Cassie stood and opened the door. "Do you need more rope?"

Will looked as if he had been awake for hours.

He scratched the back of his head. "No rope. I heard a rumor, and I wanted to investigate it."

Cassie picked a strand of her cat's yellow fur off her army green pants and pretended not to notice Will's dimples.

"Okay," she said, bracing herself. "What's the rumor?"

"The word on the street is you have secret coffee hidden somewhere."

Cassie's mouth dropped open. "Where did you hear that?"

Will leaned his arm on the doorframe. "I have my sources, and I smell the distinct scent of gourmet coffee brewing."

She crossed one hiking boot over the other. "There's coffee for everyone in the cafeteria on the table with the juice and water. Anyone is welcome to it."

Will smiled a toothy grin and leaned in toward her. He smelled like soap and mint mouthwash. "I tested that coffee, and it's not the good stuff. I think the legend of the secret coffee is true, but you're hiding it."

Cassie averted her eyes from his gaze. "What makes you think I have anything to hide?"

"Maybe you don't trust me with your special coffee."

Beth's head popped through the door beside Will's shoulder. "Hey, guys. Am I interrupting?"

"No. Will was going to get coffee from our wonderful drink table."

"Actually, we have some great coffee in my office," Beth said, pointing to her office door. "Right through there. Help yourself."

Will put his hand on Beth's shoulder but never took his eyes from Cassie. "Thank you. I'll do that."

&

The tiny concession stand made the July afternoon feel even hotter. Cassie ripped open a box of candy. During break time, campers swam, hiked, or took part in the most popular activity—hanging out in front of the snack bar to flirt. Seeing the campers try to grow up too fast frustrated Cassie. The girls wore too much makeup, and the boys competed for their attention. Cassie wanted them to focus on Bible studies, prayer time, and making friends, but she couldn't do anything but keep a close eye on them.

Cassie and Beth gathered their most useful information behind the bar while taking money and handing out sweets. If the campers noticed the adults a few feet away, they must have assumed they were there only to provide sour straws and giant pickles.

Cassie warned the counselors about plans for sneaking out of the cabins, and she often thwarted young hand-holding couples from wandering into the woods out of the watchful eye of the leaders.

Cassie unloaded a case of sodas into the refrigerator. "Why did you give Will our coffee?" she asked Beth.

Beth took a roll of gray tape from the top of the old refrigerator. "Have you ever heard the saying 'Keep your friends close and your enemies closer'?"

"I guess you're right." Cassie wiped the back of her hand across her forehead.

Beth bit a piece of tape off with her teeth and stuck it to the falling corner of a piece of poster board that listed snack prices. "But I have to say, he is charming. He complimented my french bread at lunch."

Cassie dusted the rough counter with a damp rag. "Are you sure you're not interested in him?"

"No. Why?" Beth asked. "You don't like him, do you?"

Cassie kept wiping. "He probably spends more time and money on his looks than I do."

Of course, that wasn't saying much. Today her hair was in its usual ponytail, and she was wearing one of her many pairs of cargo pants. She didn't know how any woman could go through an entire workday without pockets. But that morning she had put on a white V-neck top instead of her usual camp T-shirt.

Beth put the last few Kit Kats into a box. "I sure could use one of these right now."

Cassie wanted one, too, but it would be cruel to eat it in front of Beth. Beth hated exercise but constantly began and ended the latest fad diet. It was grapefruit one week, only bacon and eggs the next, and once she went a week and a half eating only cabbage soup. Cassie envied her friend's curves. Beth had hips and a butt, and her shirts fit just right. Cassie was built like her mother, naturally petite and thin, and way too boyish.

The bell in the yard clanged, and a group of girls in chandelier earrings and pink fingernails made their way to the snack bar. Cassie asked the girl with a short, spiky haircut which flavor of sucker she wanted, keeping her eyes on Will, who moved toward them, talking to another counselor. Her stomach tightened, but she put on a smile.

"If it isn't my two new best friends," Will said.

Beth kicked Cassie under the counter. Cassie smiled, remembering Beth's plan to keep a close watch on Will. "You were a pretty easy friend to win. All we had to do was point you in the direction of coffee."

Will pointed to the older man with him. "This is my cabinmate Roger. We've recently discovered that fourteen-year-old boys are the smelliest creatures on the face of the earth."

"Try cleaning their cabins every week," Cassie said.

Will wore swim trunks and a bright towel around his neck. "That's dedication." He laid a dollar bill on the counter. "Could Roger and I get a couple bottles of water?"

She took out the waters and wrapped paper towels around the outside. "I see you're planning to take a swim."

Will took the waters and handed one to Roger. "I saw some of the guys trying to dunk each other. We're going to show them how it's done."

When the men had walked away toward the pool, Cassie took a deep breath, trying to stay as casual as possible and not worry Beth. "Did I mention that the boss is going to be coming down to the camp next week?"

Beth, who had hopped up to sit on the edge of the chest freezer, leaned forward. "Mr. Hartley's coming here? Why? Why doesn't he send someone from his office like he usually does?"

Cassie kept her eyes on a boy and girl who had separated from the group and were sitting on the grass side by side. "I don't know. His e-mail said—"

"Wait a minute," Beth said. "He e-mailed you?"

"Yes, and he has some issues to talk to me about."

Beth swung her legs. For a moment, she looked like one of the campers. "Are you worried? I mean, he doesn't come down here unless it's something pretty big."

Cassie's head ached because of the stifling heat. She needed to lie down. She shouldn't have brought up the e-mail. "I don't think it's a big deal. I mean, he probably has to visit every camp at least once or twice a year."

An awkward silence hung between them until two boys, sweating and out of breath, ordered Gatorades.

Beth shrugged. "Sure, you're probably right. Nothing to worry about."

three

Will pushed his brother's tool belt and electric drill from the passenger seat to the dusty floorboard and climbed into Connor's four-wheel-drive pickup. "This thing's a mess."

Connor drummed his thumbs against the steering wheel. "It's a work truck. What do you expect?"

Despite their innate differences, Will and Connor made a good team. Connor handled the construction side of their real-estate business, spending his days outside the office on job sites. Will dealt with the development end, negotiating deals and looking for new projects. "This needs to be quick. I have a guy down there covering for me in a cabin full of crazed teenagers."

Connor sifted through a stack of paper on his dashboard. "It shouldn't take long. My crew can't start working on the renovation until you sign these contracts." Connor pushed a clipboard of papers and an ink pen into Will's hands.

Will read through the first page and flipped to the next. He rolled his shoulders in an attempt to relieve some of the tension that crept back into his muscles. Will loved his work, and he was good at it. But he hadn't even realized the pressure he felt from his father and their clients until he had a break from it at the camp.

"I have to hand it to you," Connor said. "You're pretty committed to your job, spending a week down there."

Will looked up from the paperwork. "What do you mean? I'm taking a week off work."

"Sure." Connor rested an arm on the open window, staring

out past the wooden SUNSET CAMP sign toward the canyon. "I just can't believe Dad talked you into doing something so crazy for a deal."

Will fought off annoyance at Connor's assumptions. "There isn't a deal right now. Dad is just interested in the place."

Connor's face creased with surprise. "I figured he put you up to this. Everybody knows the camp is on the verge of going under. Why else would you be here?"

Their father had suggested Will look into the property, but it wasn't why Will was at the camp. "The youth minister said he needed another adult to volunteer. I'm here to help out."

"Then I'm surprised Dad was so gung ho about you taking the week off work," Connor said.

Will couldn't remember the last time any of them had taken an entire week away from the business. "You have a point."

"He could be testing you. If we end up buying this place, maybe he'll let you handle more of the big contracts."

And maybe his father would stop treating Will like he was seventeen.

"Mom would be happy. That's for sure," Connor said.

Their mother had been trying to get their dad to slow down and travel more or at least stop spending sixty hours a week in the office. "I don't know. Buying this place would make perfect business sense, but right now I just want to help them get out of their mess. I'd hate to see it close."

"Uh-oh. Is my business-savvy brother turning sentimental on me?"

Will chuckled. "I wouldn't go that far, but the new director and I were reminiscing about being campers. She's pretty passionate about what they do down there, and I can't really blame her."

Connor raised a dark eyebrow. "So you're not interested in the property because of this woman?"

"It's not like that. I just met her, and apparently she's not too fond of me."

"Then she must not know you're Wyatt Bend's most eligible bachelor, or she'd be throwing herself at you like all the rest."

Will shook his head at the ribbing from his brother. "From what I can tell, she thinks I'm pretty obnoxious."

"I like her already," Connor said.

"Very funny." Will scribbled his signature and the date on the bottom line and handed the contract back to Connor. "Besides, she's not my type. Don't get me wrong. She's gorgeous in a tomboyish sort of way, but she's stubborn and unreasonable."

Connor shoved the clipboard back onto his dashboard. "Sounds exactly like the kind of girl you need to keep you in line. But if you want Dad to stop breathing down your neck every day, you'll figure out a way to make this deal happen."

❧

Cassie shone the flashlight on the path to her house. Trees hid all but the chimney of the home that sat twenty feet up the narrow road leading out of the canyon.

Inside, she turned on the radio to chase away the quietness. She didn't have a television, and in the evenings the silent house was a stark contrast to the screaming youth.

Petal, Cassie's plump yellow cat, dozed on the couch, curled up on her favorite afghan. Cassie hopped as she unlaced her hiking boots. Petal opened one eye, letting her know she had woken her.

The phone rang, and Cassie tucked it under her ear. "Hi, Mom," she said without hearing the voice on the other end of the line. Her mother called three times a week without fail before she went to bed.

"Where were you? I've been trying to call you all evening," her mother said.

Cassie plopped onto an overstuffed chair. The blanket she used to cover the ratty cushions slipped down, revealing outdated brown and orange fabric. "Mom, you know I can't always get home on time. It's not like I work a nine to five."

The sound of running water and dishes clanking came from the other end of the phone. Since her father had left when Cassie was ten years old, her mother had lived alone. Most likely she had cooked for Cassie's sister, Melissa; Melissa's accountant husband; and the couple's two girls, but Cassie was too stubborn to ask about her sister. She wasn't in the mood to hear her mother talk about Melissa and her perfect life.

"Honey, I know you don't work a normal job, but maybe that's the problem."

"Not tonight, Mom."

The sound of running water stopped. "I'm worried about you."

Petal jumped into Cassie's lap. When Cassie had taken over as director, the cat had shown up at the kitchen door. She purred and pressed her paws into Cassie's leg. "There's nothing to worry about. I'm fine."

Cassie and her mother had had this conversation a hundred times before, and Cassie couldn't figure out how to keep from repeating it. She closed her eyes to prepare for what was next.

"How are you going to meet a husband if you spend all your time working?"

There it was. The question she hated most, even more than, "When are you going to get a real job?" Cassie held her breath.

"Cassie? Are you still there?"

She tapped the phone against her forehead then held the phone back up to her face. "I'm still here, Mom."

"I want you to settle down like Melissa. She is your *baby* sister."

Petal lifted her chin in the air when Cassie scratched her neck. "It's not like twenty-seven is ancient. A lot of women have careers before they have families." This argument was impossible to win.

"Honey, if you want a career, go back to managing a restaurant."

Cassie had worked in the restaurant business after college graduation, managing an upscale restaurant in Albuquerque. The hours were hard, but no worse than what she was doing now. The pay was great, but her heart wasn't in it. When she turned down a promotion and returned to Sunset Camp, her family and friends told her she was crazy.

"Use the degree you earned," her mom said. "What you're doing isn't a career. You're still at summer camp."

Her mother's words hurt. She had spent every summer at the camp from the time she was in junior high, first as a camper and later as an employee during college between semesters. She had lived in the tiny workers' cabin with other students. When she accepted the assistant director position, it was like coming home. Now she served as the interim director, and she didn't want anything to ruin her opportunity.

"I never would have let you go down there when you were twelve if I had known it would become your whole life."

Coming back with all her usual defenses was pointless. Cassie didn't bother pointing out she was a director, the youngest and only woman camp director in the state, even if it was only temporary. Explaining that she was making a difference in kids' lives by bringing them closer to God wouldn't even help her argument. She'd tried them all before.

"I just don't want you to end up single because you think

every man is going to leave you like your father."

Cassie cringed. Her mother reserved mention of Cassie's father for when she really wanted to make a point. The last time Cassie had heard from him was a year ago when he told her he was marrying a casino waitress in Las Vegas.

"Can we drop it?" Cassie asked.

Her mother was quiet for a moment. "I'll leave you alone," she said in a serious tone, "when you move back to New Mexico, meet a nice man, and have a couple of my grandbabies."

"Oh. . .just that."

Her mom laughed. "Good night, honey. You need to get your rest."

Cassie stopped scratching Petal's neck, and a fat orange tail hit the phone.

"What was that?"

"Oh nothing. Only Petal saying good night."

"Good night." Cassie heard the exasperation in her mother's voice.

Some days, especially paydays, she didn't know if moving to Oklahoma had been the right decision, but when she saw the difference in the kids after a week at the camp or when she woke up early to go on a hike up the canyon, she remembered why she was there.

Now she feared it might all be taken away from her.

four

A steady thumping in her head woke Cassie. She struggled to open her eyes and focus them on the glow of her alarm clock: 1:38 a.m. Her fingers fumbled for the aspirin in her nightstand drawer, but the banging returned.

The front door. She grabbed a sweatshirt off the back of the chair and pulled it over her tank top and pajama bottoms.

The banging on the door got louder and caused her head to throb even more. Someone was losing patience.

"I'm coming," she yelled. "Hang on."

Through the peephole, she saw a chin and a neck but no face. "Who is it?"

"It's me," Will said.

She placed her hand on the doorknob but stopped. "This is the second time you've woken me up since we've met."

"Cassie, I need your help. Please open the door."

The shakiness in his voice made her throw the door open.

He stepped inside the entryway, his face pale and his lips tight. "A couple of my boys are missing."

The fog of sleepiness lifted from Cassie. "What? How?"

"They're gone," he said. "I'm such a light sleeper. I don't know how it could have happened."

Cassie didn't need to hear any more. She was already pulling on her hiking boots with her pajama pants.

"I'm sorry to wake you, but I figured you might know where to look. Should we call the cops? Should I wake up the other counselors?"

She almost enjoyed seeing Mr. Calm frazzled, not knowing

what to do next. Unfortunately, there was no time to revel in the moment. "I'm sure they just snuck out. Don't worry. We'll find them."

"Should we check if anyone else is missing?" Will asked.

"Not yet. If we wake up the counselors, the campers are going to wake up, too."

A few minutes later, Cassie knocked on the door of Beth's one-room cabin, and soon Beth's face was peering out the window. Her eyes were hardly open, and her forehead was scrunched like a shar-pei's. She opened the door wearing a robe and carrying a baseball bat.

"Expecting someone?" Cassie asked.

Beth held her hand over her heart. "I watched a movie about a stalker before I went to bed."

Cassie took the baseball bat from Beth and leaned it on the front porch. "We have some boys out of their cabin. Can you help us look?"

"Of course. Let me change out of my pj's."

"Will and I will check the hiking paths. You check the other popular places." Cassie motioned for Will to follow her.

"I'll be right behind you," Beth said, going back into her cabin.

Cassie headed across the open grassy area to the canyon wall on the other side of the tabernacle. She trudged under the weight of her sweatshirt and dreaded the march through the wilderness with Will Overman. On the other hand, being with Will could possibly bring her some insight into his motives, but she'd need to be careful not to give up any information about the camp.

Will jogged to catch up to her. "Did you say we're going hiking?"

"We have to whisper, and please, trust me," Cassie said, not wanting the missing campers to hide from them. "I've done this before, and they are almost always at one of a few places." Cassie pointed the unlit flashlight at the canyon wall. "The top of the canyon is one of them."

"You're suggesting we hike up the canyon with only that little flashlight?" Will asked.

"No. We won't use the flashlight until we find them. We don't want them to spot us before we see them." Cassie concealed her smile. "You're not afraid of the dark, are you?"

"Afraid of the dark?" Will stepped in front of her. "I'll lead."

It didn't take them long to reach the open gazebo behind the tabernacle. Small groups met there when they didn't mind going without air-conditioning, which wasn't often these days. When Cassie had been a camper, nothing in the camp had been air conditioned except the nurse's station. Campers would fake headaches for the chance to lie on a cot in the cool room.

Trees and plants hid the opening to the trail behind the gazebo, and Will walked back and forth searching for it.

"Need help?" Cassie asked. The search would go faster if he would let her take the lead.

"No, I know it's right here. . .somewhere."

She would have forced him to ask her for help, but the teens were wandering around by themselves. She cleared her throat, and he motioned for her to go ahead of him. She found the path immediately, and they hiked silently, listening for voices or footsteps.

Darkness fell around them. The trees blocked the moonlight, and the lights from the buildings and cabins were out of sight. Luckily, every turn, every tree stump, and every rock were familiar to Cassie.

"Are you up for a shortcut?" she asked, eager to test Will.

Will sighed. "I am if you are."

The steeper, more difficult path was on their left, and it inclined almost straight up. A rope had been secured to a tree at the top of the slope to make it possible for hikers to pull themselves up the slick rocks. Cassie jerked the rope to make sure it was secured tightly. "Hold on to this," Cassie said, handing him the rope.

Will reached through the darkness, first touching his hand to hers, then taking the rope.

"This will lead us the entire way, but the stone under your feet is going to be slippery, so watch your footing," she said.

Will didn't respond. She felt him pull at the rope behind her.

They worked together silently. When Cassie fought to scale a boulder, Will put his hand on her elbow. She felt as if she were climbing blindfolded, but she let the rope lead her up the canyon. After several minutes, she reached the trail, and she gave Will a hand as he maneuvered the final step.

"Thanks," he said, his hand still wrapped around hers.

Cassie pulled it away, spun around, and pretended not to notice how effortlessly he made it up the rocks.

"We're almost there," Cassie said. "One more incline to go, which will seem like a cakewalk compared to this."

The main trail stretched in front of them, and with no trees above them now, the moonlight lit their way. A rustling came from the bushes beside them. They stayed motionless as they listened. "Cooper? Seth?" Will whispered.

Will and Cassie both jumped when a gray armadillo popped out of the leaves. It turned and ran at the sight of them.

Cassie couldn't help but laugh. Will playfully slugged her on the arm before laughing with her. "I hope I can make this hike sometime when I'll have a chance to enjoy it instead of searching for bandits. It's actually pretty beautiful up here at night."

The sandy rocks of the canyon left orange stains across his

white T-shirt, and beads of sweat glistened on his forehead.

They reached the highest point of the canyon wall, and the cloudless night gave them a blanket of stars. It was nights like this that made Cassie wonder how anyone could not believe in God.

She ran her hand across the boulder covered with carved names and initials. At one time she hiked to this spot every morning to pray. She felt close to God when she was there, but now she struggled to escape from work.

"I guess they're not here." Will turned back toward the trail. "I hope Beth is having better luck."

A piece of paper caught Cassie's eye. "Hang on." She leaned over and grabbed a sticky wrapper from the ice cream sandwiches Beth had planned to serve the next night. "Whoever was here raided our kitchen first."

Will took the wrapper. "But it would have been impossible for them to come down the canyon. Surely we would have seen or heard them."

"Not if they went down the other way."

Will scratched the back of his head. "I remember going down that way when I was a camper."

"So you remember how steep it is."

He nodded. "But the caves below the summit are pretty cool. If I were the boys, I'd want to see it at night. You better lead the way though. It has been years since I've done this."

It had been a long time since Cassie had hiked the back trail, too. She had never attempted it in the dark, but she would never admit that to Will.

Cassie poked around the wall of bushes and branches. When she found the narrow opening, Will walked close behind her.

❧

Will followed Cassie's loose ponytail as they trekked down

the rocky path. A few days ago Will couldn't have imagined he would be hiking in the middle of the night with someone like Cassie.

She was different than the girls he grew up with in Wyatt Bend. Fiercely independent, she challenged him at every turn.

"So, how long have you been director here? Six months?" he whispered, so the boys, wherever they were, wouldn't hear him.

Cassie glanced at him over her shoulder. "Actually, it's been about nine."

Will reached over her head to pull up a branch hanging in her path. "So how's it going?"

There was a long pause. "It's fine."

Not exactly the response he had hoped for. Will wanted more. Not so he could report back to his dad, but because he wanted to know more about her. "Do you like your job?"

Cassie stopped and turned around to face him. "I love it."

He squinted, trying to see through the shadows to the emotion on her face.

Cassie crossed her arms. "What about you? Do you like your business?"

Will took a step back. "For the most part, I do love being in real estate. It's never dull."

"What are you working on right now?" Cassie asked.

His pulse quickened as he recalled the conversation with his brother. "We have some projects in progress, but I don't know what's next."

Cassie turned back around, walking faster as the path widened in front of them. Something rustled the grass alongside the trail, but this time Cassie didn't stop to investigate.

They reached a point in the path where they had to slide down a ten-foot slope. Cassie lay down feetfirst with her stomach to the stone. She descended with a small groan and wiped off the front of her sweatshirt. Will followed. As he and Cassie walked together, a low rumble cut through the whisper of the breeze against the leaves.

Voices. Relief washed over Will.

He gripped Cassie's shoulder. She pulled it away, but as the voices grew louder, she froze.

Cassie took off toward a small overhang of the cliff wall. Will reached an arm out in front of her. "Wait," he whispered. "Can I handle this?"

Cassie handed him the flashlight and moved off the path, letting Will pass by her.

Will ran his hand along the rock wall, following the voices and feeling his way into the dark cave.

"What time is it?" a girl asked.

Sneaking out to meet girls. He should have known.

"I don't know," another said. "But what do you think the counselors would say if they found out we snuck out of our bunks?"

The high-pitched giggles of teenage girls rang out through the darkness. Will clicked his flashlight on and shone it on his face.

The teens screamed.

Will aimed the light at the boys' stunned expressions. "I would probably say it was irresponsible, immature, and dangerous."

Will turned the light toward the teens. Whitney, one of the members of his church's youth group, sat with her mouth open. "What are you doing out here?" He followed her gaze with his flashlight. "Marcy, you, too? You guys are in so much trouble."

Cassie moved out of the shadows to the path in front of them.

"Because of you, three people had to get out of bed to search for you in the dark." Will's voice boomed against the canyon walls as he shone the light in each of the four stunned faces. "This means I'll be extremely grumpy in the morning when determining your punishment."

The guys groaned. Whitney's lip quivered.

"You're not going to call my mom are you?" Cooper asked.

"Oh man, my mom would kill me," Seth said.

He had found their weak points—Mom. He would remember that and use it to get through the week.

Marcy stood from a rock and pointed at the boy in the cap. "You promised me we wouldn't get caught."

Will looked down at the other teens sitting on the rocks. "I think this should be a lesson to you to make your own decisions and not let other people talk you into doing things you shouldn't."

Cassie cleared her throat. Will turned around to see her swirling her finger. Time to wrap it up.

"Okay, let's head back to camp," Will said. "You guys have been out too long as it is."

Will and Cassie followed behind the teens, like guards escorting prisoners.

"I can't believe the girls from my church would sneak out," Will said to Cassie.

Cassie shrugged. "I know, but at least we found them. We'll get them back where they belong."

"Do you think Beth is still looking?" Will asked.

"I'll call her on her cell phone and get the girls back to their cabins," Cassie said. "You can make sure the guys are back in their bunks. Then let's meet at the pool just to make sure no one had any problems."

They parted ways at the tabernacle. The boys shuffled their feet as they walked.

"So, come on, guys. You have to tell me how you did it," Will said.

"Huh?" Seth asked.

"How did you sneak out?"

The boys looked at each other and then at their tennis shoes.

"WD-40," Cooper said. "We sprayed the hinges on the door earlier today."

A few minutes later, after Will had returned the boys to the cabin and arrived at the pool, a slender hand dangled an ice cream sandwich in front of his face. Will looked up from where he sat at the edge of the pool. "You sure know the way to a man's heart."

He moved his shoes to the other side so Cassie could sit beside him.

Her bare feet slipped into the water, and she gave a satisfied sigh. Will studied her as he unwrapped his ice cream. Her face looked soft and smooth, and she finally acted more relaxed around him—not the same defensive girl she had been.

He pointed to the plastic bag in her hand. "You're eating carrots. . .instead of ice cream?"

She smiled and held up another sandwich. "No, I have a sweet tooth, but Beth would hate it if I brought her ice cream and she had to turn it down. I didn't want her to feel left out."

"That was nice." He took a big bite of the already-melting ice cream.

She shrugged. "She would do it for me."

The camp was quiet except for the sound of their legs swishing in the water. He couldn't remember the last time he had sat in silence, enjoying the evening. And he couldn't have shared it with a better person. He liked Cassie. Sure, she could be brash and unpredictable, but she was also captivating. "I wanted to tell you thank you," he said, crumpling the wrapper in one hand.

"For what?"

"For helping me tonight. I was pretty panicked when I knocked on your door."

Cassie laughed. "You did look white as a ghost."

He tossed the ball of paper into the trash can behind him. "I'm usually pretty calm under pressure, but I didn't want to call someone's parents and tell them their kid had been eaten by a mountain lion."

"Yeah," she said. "Wouldn't be very good for my career either."

He nudged her with his elbow. "I'm serious. You really helped me out tonight. You're great at what you do."

"Thanks. I had a pretty good sidekick with me."

The chain-link gate to the pool squeaked. He turned to see Beth walking toward them.

Cassie pulled her legs out of the water and stood, stretching her arms above her head. "I'm exhausted. It's time to get some rest."

Cassie looked beautiful with the blue moonlight on her face and her defenses down. Will swallowed hard, trying to extinguish the spark he felt. His last girlfriend called it quits because of his commitment to his business. Experience told Will that acting on his interest in Cassie would lead to heartache for both of them. If he decided to please his dad and pursue purchasing the camp, feelings for Cassie would only make things more complicated.

five

Cassie held her hand to her nose as she stepped into cabin fourteen. The overwhelming smell of mildew made her empty stomach churn. She had skipped breakfast to get an early start. The small cabin hadn't been used all season because it was in desperate need of repair. She had run the numbers on hiring someone to do the work, but as usual the camp couldn't afford it.

She slid on her work gloves and pulled back the corner of orange carpet, revealing a dusty pad underneath. She groaned as she rolled the heavy mass to the middle of the room.

"Sorry to interrupt, but it looks like you could use some help," a deep voice said.

She looked up to see Will standing in the open doorway. Clean-shaven and bright-eyed, he didn't look like he had been up half the night.

Cassie pushed a strand of hair off her face with the back of her gloved hand. "That's nice of you, but you have other commitments right now as a counselor."

"Actually, I wasn't talking about me." He stepped inside the door and revealed the four offenders from the night before who stood on the front porch. "Their youth pastors had conversations with them about their poor choices and told me you have some volunteers to help out this morning."

Cassie couldn't deny that it was a good plan. She dug in her toolbox for gloves. "I could use a couple of extra sets of hands in here. We could use a couple of people in the kitchen, too."

"Awesome," Whitney said. "I thought I was going to have to work in here."

Cassie tossed her a pair of the gloves. "The guys can help Beth in the kitchen. She always needs vegetables chopped and trays served. The girls can work with me today."

"Ah, man," Cooper said. "We really have to work in the kitchen?"

Will winked at Cassie. "You heard her, guys. Let's go."

"This stinks," Seth said.

"I know. I know. She's tough." Will pointed at the two girls. "We'll see you back with the group later."

The girls with their polished nails and cute clothes joined Cassie in the middle of the room. "Who's going to get this gross carpet out of here?" Marcy asked.

"I had been wondering that myself until you two showed up," Cassie said.

Whitney used an elastic band around her wrist to pull her hair into a ponytail, leaving a big loop of hair on the back of her head. "Are you serious? This will take us all day."

Cassie didn't answer. Instead she pointed the girls to a corner of the carpet. They stared at her like she was going to tell them it was all a big joke and they were really going out for pedicures and facials.

"We're going to gut this cabin," Cassie said to blank stares. "The three of us, together. Now grab the end of the carpet."

The girls looked at each other. Their feet stayed glued to the ground. Whitney put her hands on her hips. "I threw my elbow out in tennis this season. I don't think my coach would want me to hurt it again."

Marcy nodded. "And I've been having some woman issues. I need to ask the nurse for a painkiller."

Cassie shrugged and concealed the oncoming laughter at

their feeble attempts to get out of the job. "Whatever you think is best."

The girls looked at each other and turned to leave.

"But you know, when I said that you were going to help me, one of those guys you hang out with rolled his eyes."

Whitney spun around. "Which one?"

"Does it matter? I'm pretty sure they think you girls are too weak to help me out. I guess I'll go get the guys and let you two work in the kitchen for the day."

The girls glared at each other. Whitney marched to the center of the room and wrapped her arms around the huge roll of dirty carpet. Marcy's shoulders fell as she bent over to help her. Together they dragged it toward the door.

With the carpet finally on the front porch of the cabin, the girls stood a little taller with their hands on their hips. They surveyed what they had done, both covered in dust and sweat.

"Time to demolish the bathroom," Cassie said.

The girls scrunched their button noses but didn't question her. They deserved a treat for being good sports. Their faces beamed when Cassie held up a sledgehammer.

The girls didn't grumble as they pulled the two toilets out of the cabin and didn't run when a mouse scurried across the now-bare concrete floor.

After the trio had carried the rest of the junk to the dumpster and ripped out part of the bathroom, Beth brought them each a sandwich, chips, and a thermos of lemonade for lunch. The girls found a spot on the grass outside the cabin while Cassie and Beth sat on the railing of the porch. Cassie took a gulp of lemonade.

"It looked like you and Mr. Big Shot hit it off last night," Beth said.

Cassie shielded her eyes from the sun. "I don't know. I

mean, sometimes Will's a decent guy, and then I remember he might be trying to take our camp. I can't let my guard down."

Beth's eyebrows arched.

"You know what I mean. I know I'll be the one who loses in all of this." Cassie dug through her bag of food. "Did you bring dessert?"

Beth held up a napkin with two chocolate chip cookies.

"You're the best," Cassie said.

Beth nodded toward the two girls, who were now lying on their backs staring up at the cloudless sky. "I didn't want the two fugitives to get them."

Cassie closed her eyes as she bit into a cookie. "They aren't such bad kids," she said with a mouthful.

"Yeah, the guys have actually been pretty fun to have around today. They've nicknamed me the Dining Room Diva," Beth said, beaming.

"The Dining Room Diva," Cassie said. "I like it." Cassie paused and glanced at the girls.

"Those two actually surprised me today. I think they surprised themselves, too." Like she'd told Beth, they were good girls, just too willing to please cute young boys.

After sending the pair back to their group and running to her house for a quick shower, Cassie walked to her office on leaden legs. Her old office chair never looked so good. She dropped into the seat and rubbed her palms across her achy thighs. She had worked the girls harder than she had realized. Eager to stay in her office and rest for a few minutes, she opened her e-mail.

Her sister's name was in the list of e-mail senders. They rarely spoke, only having information about their lives relayed by their mother with excruciating pride. Melissa constantly sent her forwards, which Cassie automatically deleted. They usually had subject lines like "A Poem of Friendship" or "Please Keep This Going." But today the subject line read, "Hey, Sis!" Cassie opened it.

> *Hi.*
>
> *Mom says you're busy with work. The girls are doing great. Gracie already knows all of her letters, and Ashley rolled over before any of the children in our playgroup. Thanks for sending the books for Gracie's birthday. Daniel got a big new account at work last week. A promotion is on the horizon. I'm as busy as ever, heading up the new children's fair at our church.*
>
> *I attached an article I read from one of my e-newsletters. I thought you might find it helpful.*
>
> > *Talk to you soon.*
> > *Melissa*

Cassie blinked. Despite the incessant bragging about her perfect family, she liked hearing about her nieces' achievements—as long as it didn't include one of her sister's usual digs. But there was no mention of Cassie's messy house, and Melissa didn't point out that she was single. It was nice.

She clicked on the icon of a paper clip, opening the attachment on the e-mail. Had she underestimated her sister all these years? Maybe her sensitivity—okay, defensiveness— toward anything involving her sister contributed to their strained relationship.

She enlarged the screen to see the headline of the article, which read, "Women in Their 20s: Sabotaging Happiness?" Cassie leaned closer to the screen, hoping she had misread the headline. She read the second line, "Are women today ruining their chances for a happy home life and a family by putting their careers above their roles as wives and mothers?"

She turned away from the computer. Her chest tingled with her vibrating heart. Is that what her sister thought of her, that she didn't want to be happy?

Cassie needed a distraction. So she did the one thing that helped her forget her problems. She worked. She usually made a point to stay out of the kitchen, but today she wasn't worried about being in the way. Cassie wasn't known for her culinary skills, but she liked to get her hands dirty.

Beth didn't comment when Cassie looped the apron strap over her head. "What can I do for you, boss?" she asked Beth.

Beth's green eyes danced. "Oh, I get to be the boss for the rest of the day? I have some ideas."

Cassie scrubbed her hands with soap and water. "I'm serious. I'm here to help. What do you need me to do?"

Beth looked her up and down. "I need all of these onions chopped, but I don't have time to take you to the emergency room tonight."

A timer rang, and Cassie turned it off. "You've seen me use a chain saw. I didn't hurt myself then."

Beth took a huge pan of lemon bars out of the oven. "Yes, but do you remember the incident with the spork?"

Beth would never let her live down the time she made herself bleed with a plastic spoon with little fork tines on the end. At a picnic, the spork had snapped in half as she tried to eat a slice of watermelon. The plate on her lap had slid onto the ground, and the sharp plastic scraped her leg.

"I would hardly call it an incident. I didn't bleed much, and it was a plastic utensil."

"My point exactly," Beth said.

Cassie pulled a knife from a drawer, and Beth took two steps backward with her back against the oven, her eyes wide with feigned terror.

"Don't worry. I'm fine," Cassie said. Her voice grew serious.

"I need you to let me do this."

Beth threw her hands up in the air. "Be my guest."

It took Cassie a few minutes to find the cutting board. She set up shop on an empty corner of counter space. Before long, her eyes burned from the onions. Tears ran down her cheeks and dripped onto her shirt. She looked up at the ceiling, trying to get the stinging to subside. She wiped her face with the bottom of her apron.

Her eyes stung, and she couldn't see what she was chopping. She felt the edge of the blade sink into the tip of her finger. She whimpered.

Beth ran over, and when her eyes looked down toward the red blood, she screamed. Beth pulled her over to the utility sink and turned on the faucet. The cold water blasted against the gash.

"I'm okay. I'm okay," Cassie said. "It's not that bad."

Beth pulled Cassie's hand out of the water and examined it, but again, blood came through the skin. "I knew I shouldn't have let you have the knife, especially while you're so upset."

Cassie pulled her bleeding finger away from Beth. "What do you mean?"

Beth wrapped a dishrag around her finger. "You know I love you, but you've been acting kind of out of it these last few days."

Cassie let her head drop. "I thought I was hiding it pretty well."

Beth took a butterfly bandage out of the old metal first-aid box bolted to the wall. "I think you're going to get by without stitches, but you should know you can't hide that kind of thing from me, not that you've been doing a very good job at it."

Cassie was too tired to protest as Beth squeezed anti-bacterial ointment on the wound and pulled the bandage around it. Cassie squirmed. "I know. I don't know what's going on with me. My sister has always driven me crazy. I knew when I took this job it was meant to be temporary and the camp was struggling. None of this is new."

Beth dipped her chin to her throat. "You know that I'm worried about you."

Cassie slid the onion she had been chopping from the cutting board to the trash can. "I'll be fine. I'm just a little stressed out. I'll be fine."

"You already said that," Beth said with a grin.

"I know. If I say it enough times, it will be true."

❧

After dinner Cassie mopped the floor and helped Beth with the dishes. It felt good to lose herself in the rhythms of work. Cassie sent Beth home early and put the last load of dishes through the industrial dishwasher. She turned out lights in the dining area and rolled the mop into the storage closet. The cafeteria door slammed, and she poked her head out of the closet. "Beth?"

Will stepped into the light of the kitchen and pointed to the mop. "I see you got a promotion."

She dusted off the front of her shirt and pants. "Funny."

"How were the girls today?" Will asked.

"Great. We had fun."

"If that was fun, I would love to see your idea of hard work."

He lifted his arm and scratched the back of his head. "It seems like I'm asking you for help a lot, doesn't it?"

"What now?"

He chuckled. "Don't worry. It's not serious."

The closet door closed behind her with a *click*. "What is it? What happened?"

He rubbed the stubble appearing on his chin. "There is a boy walking around camp without any underwear."

"Someone lost his underwear," she said.

"No," he said. "It's more like he had his underwear stolen."

Not knowing what else to say, she said, "Like some sort of animal came in and took them?"

"Not unless there are bears around here that take boxers and string them up on the flagpole," Will said with a stern expression.

A laugh burst out of Cassie's lips. She walked to the window. Sure enough, a strand of boxers, one tied to another, fluttered in the breeze. She loved that things really hadn't changed much from when she was a camper.

"And what's the problem?" Cassie asked. "Deciding who's going to touch them to get them down from there?"

He wrapped a hand around her shoulder. At first she tensed, but the moment was so light, she couldn't help but relax under his arm. "This is where you come in. Apparently whoever did this was a Boy Scout or something because none of us can figure out how to get the weird knot he tied undone. Do you mind if we cut the rope?"

"Let me take a look at it first."

A crowd gathered underneath the flying boxer shorts. Cassie inspected the flagpole. Instead of wrapping the rope around the cleat, someone had tied the rope in a complicated knot around the bracket. The pranksters got extra points for their ingenuity.

Cassie quickly untied the knot. A few campers groaned when she pulled the boxers down, apparently disappointed they weren't going to be left to fly over the camp all night. The boxers were made from patterned materials, one with tiny golfers and another with yellow smiley faces.

"I think we've had enough fun for tonight," Will announced. "Everyone needs to head to their cabins."

The group dispersed into smaller groups and headed

toward the boys' and girls' sides of the camp. Will spun around with his finger in the air. "Oh. . .and if anyone hears about plans to sneak out, ask them to talk to one of the four who had to work today."

Cassie picked up a stick at the edge of the grass. She hooked a pair of boxers lying on the ground to the end of it. She held it away from herself toward Will. "Boxers up the flagpole. An oldie but a goody."

He didn't take the underwear. "It was pretty good, but you're crazy if you think I'm touching those."

"Hold this," she said, thrusting the stick in his hand. She marched back into the cafeteria.

When she returned with a black trash bag, Will still stood on the lawn, holding the stick awkwardly away from his body. Cassie opened the bag with a flourish.

"So how did you know how to get the knot untied?" he asked.

Cassie held the bag open and nodded at Will to drop the underwear inside. "My little sister and I were in Girl Scouts together. I got the badge."

He shook the stick until he heard the boxers hit the bottom of the plastic sack. "I guess the Boy Scout comment was a little sexist. Do you have any other siblings?"

She took a deep breath in through her nose, fighting down the emotions of her sister's snarky e-mail. "Just the one." One was enough for her to handle. "And I probably shouldn't call her my little sister anymore. She has two kids and a husband."

"It's okay. My siblings still call me the baby of the family."

Cassie could have guessed he was the youngest. He stood before her dressed like a teenager in basketball sneakers, long shorts, and a baseball cap. "Let me guess. Your parents were easier on you than your siblings, and you could usually charm your way out of anything."

"Fair enough," Will said. "That sounds about right."

Cassie held the long stick out in front of her and tried to scoop the second pair of boxers onto the end. When the tip dug into the grass, she pushed harder. "And you never take anything too seriously."

The stick broke free from the ground and sent the boxers flying toward Will. He didn't duck fast enough, and the underwear struck the side of his head. Cassie instantly dropped the stick and clasped her hands over her mouth.

He looked up at her with his eyes wide. "You did that on purpose."

Her cheeks warmed. "I didn't. I promise. I'm so sorry."

He playfully kicked the underwear lying on the grass toward her. She ran to keep them from hitting her leg. When Will dropped the last pair in the bag, he tied a knot in the top of it. "I guess I'd better figure out who these belong to."

"You never told me how many siblings you have," she said.

"There are five of us, three boys and two girls."

She envisioned them around the table with the turkey in the Norman Rockwell painting. "Are you all close?"

He stopped to think about it. "You know what, we are close. I work with my brother and my sister. I even talk to my sister in Florida pretty regularly. I feel really blessed to have my family around."

Cassie couldn't explain why, but Will's words felt like a slug to the stomach. She crossed her arms. "You're really lucky," she managed out of her mouth. "It sounds perfect."

Will leaned on the flagpole. "Oh it's definitely not perfect. We can argue with the best of them. And there's Brendan, my middle brother. He left town and never looked back."

"He sounds like me," Cassie said.

"You and your family aren't close?"

"We're probably the opposite of your family. Someone looking at us from the outside would say that when we're together, it seems"—Cassie struggled for the right word—"pleasant. But in reality, there are all these things there, under the surface."

He opened his eyes wide. "It must be hard."

She nodded her head as they silently walked down the gravel road dividing the common area from the boys' cabins. Cassie breathed in the sweet night air to calm what was inside her head. She looked up toward her house.

Music and voices drifted out of the windows of the cabins. Will lifted the trash bag in the direction of a cabin. "This is my stop. Home sweet home."

"Cabin number five," she said. "Nice." It was the only one with all new mattresses without the plastic coverings.

"The boys say we're the coolest group. I can't help but agree."

A roar of laughter came from the cabin. Will walked backward. "I'd better get in there. Who knows what they're up to. I need to do our nightly devotion and get to bed."

"Good night," Cassie said, but it came out barely a whisper as he turned and walked away from her.

I hope you're here for the right reasons, Will Overman.

six

The two teams of teenage boys broke into huddles. Will was a foot taller than several of his teammates, made up of freshman and sophomore campers.

He gave each boy in his huddle a high five before breaking out of the circle. His team lined up to play defense against the junior and senior boys. When the center hiked the football, Will broke through the middle of the line and ran toward the quarterback, a lanky boy with long hair falling in his eyes.

Will tugged on the handkerchief hanging from the boy's waist, but it didn't budge. He pulled harder, only to see it knotted around his belt loop.

Will's teammates yelled, "Hey, that's not fair. They're trying to cheat."

The boy shook his hair out of his eyes as Will crouched low to the ground, ready to tackle.

"Uh-oh," the boy said, chucking the ball into the grass and running.

Will caught him, grabbed him, and fell to the ground, pulling the boy with him. They both landed with a hard *thud* on the grass still wet with dew.

His team cheered, and the boys ran and jumped on top of the two who were lying on the ground. Will pinned the boy down while he unknotted the handkerchief and held it triumphantly in the air.

Out of the corner of his eye, he spotted Cassie holding her hand above her brow, blocking the sun as she watched them play.

"Do you want to play another one?" asked the teen who had been tackled to the ground.

Will slapped the shoulder of a boy with a baseball cap. "You guys better take a break after that beating. Besides, it looks like somebody's waiting for me."

As he walked toward her, he couldn't stop thinking about how adorable she was. Cassie ran her fingers down a smooth ponytail.

"Don't stop on my account," she said, waving her hands in front of her. "I can wait."

He leaned in close to her ear. "Don't tell them, but I'm exhausted. I think I broke my back."

She pursed her lips and locked them with an imaginary key. "What's up?"

"I wanted to ask if you've heard anything about who started this prank war."

One innocent prank wasn't exactly what Will would dub a war. "You mean the boxers up the flagpole?"

Cassie's eyes squinted. "You haven't seen the pool?"

Will shook his head.

Her lips pursed. "Come take a look."

He followed her through the chain-link gate to the pool, which looked like it was full of strawberry Kool-Aid. Will cupped a handful of pink water and let it slip through his fingers. To be honest, it was pretty funny. If he had thought of it, he probably would've tried something like it during his camp years, but he knew better than to say that to Cassie. "I didn't hear a peep about it from the kids."

"How do a bunch of high-school kids figure out how to dye an entire swimming pool pink?"

Will stood and wiped the sweat from his forehead with his T-shirt. "The Internet."

Cassie put her hands on her hips. "We're going to have to

shut the pool down until we can test it and give it time to clear up."

"Well, that's the perfect punishment," Will said. "The other campers won't be happy when they find out the pool is closed. Whoever did it won't hear the end of it."

"I love that they're having fun," Cassie said. "I really do, but I'm worried it's going to get out of hand. I just don't want bigger pranks to cost the camp time or money. I've asked the dean to address it tonight at the worship service."

The stress on Cassie's pinched face was obviously about more than a couple of pranks. Maybe Will's father was right and the camp was in danger of closing sooner than Will had expected. Right now Will didn't care about business. He just wanted to wrap his arms around Cassie.

"I've been asking some of the counselors to keep an extra eye out tonight," Cassie said. "Especially since it's the last night of camp."

His time in the canyon, and with Cassie, was almost over. Tomorrow he'd be back in the real world, and he had some big decisions to make.

&

The final evening worship service was held in the tabernacle. Cassie attended as she always did. They were usually beautiful services, preparing the teens to go back into the world with all they had learned from their week at camp.

She hung in the back, out of the way. The dean of the camp, a pastor from a church a couple of hours away, had broken the entire camp into small circles throughout the room. The lights were dimmed, and he passed around bowls, pitchers of water, and towels. The pastor read aloud from the book of John about the Lord's Supper. "After that, he poured water into a basin," he read, "and began to wash his disciples' feet, drying them with the towel that was wrapped around him."

She watched as each counselor in a circle of campers took the feet of the camper beside them and poured the water over their bare feet. The counselor then passed the bowl of water to the next teen, who washed the feet of another camper in the circle.

Cassie, who had never been a crier, had to swallow the huge lump in her throat. Obviously the symbolism wasn't lost on the young campers; many of them were crying and others hugged after their feet had been cleaned.

For a moment she felt she was intruding. It was such an intimate setting with a guitarist playing quietly in the background. As she turned to leave, Will appeared in front of her, his feet bare.

"May I wash your feet?" Will asked.

"Excuse me?"

He held up a towel and a large bowl of water. "May I?"

Cassie let out the breath she had been holding. His eyes were soft and sincere. She wanted to trust him. But how could she? "I was just leaving."

She started to walk away, but he placed his hand on her arm. "Come on, Cassie. Let me do this."

"This is for the campers," she protested.

"Cassie, it's okay," he said in a soft voice, giving her chills on her neck.

The other adults carried their shoes in their arms. She searched for a way out, but before she could come up with an excuse, she heard herself whisper, "Okay."

Cassie followed him to a chair against the back wall. She sat down, pulled off her shoes, and slid the socks from her feet. He set the bowl of water on the concrete floor. She reluctantly slipped her feet into the bowl. She looked around to see if anyone was watching. She couldn't bring herself to look at Will. How could she let him do this? It was so unnatural for her. She wasn't comfortable sitting in the chair as Will took a pitcher from the chair beside her and poured the water over her feet. "God bless you," he said, looking up to her eyes.

"Thank you, Will," she said, her defenses melting.

&

The final day of camp was always hectic. Campers gathered e-mail addresses from friends, packed their suitcases, and rolled up their sleeping bags. Many of them had other campers sign their camp T-shirts with permanent markers.

Cassie searched the grounds for any signs of another prank, but everything was in its place. The cafeteria was especially noisy, filled with excited chatter.

Cassie struggled to concentrate as she spent the morning glued to her clipboard, checking off names as friendly youth ministers and church volunteers dragged suitcases out of the cabins and loaded teary-eyed youths into vans. An intense week of growth for a teenager was equivalent to years spent with someone in the real world.

When the final van had driven through the camp and up the steep road out of the canyon, Cassie noticed a silver two-door car parked in front of cabin five, but she didn't stop to investigate.

She and her staff would spend the rest of the day cleaning the camp—the most difficult job being the cabin bathrooms used by teenage boys without their mothers to monitor them. She headed toward the chapel, a one-room A-frame structure.

Many used the chapel for a prayer room or a place for Bible study and meditation. The entire room could seat less than twenty people. The outside had been painted barn red like the other buildings, but the inside was bare pine. The sunlight shone through the stained-glass windows.

Cassie busied herself sweeping and mopping the concrete floor and nailing a loose board back in place. With those tasks completed, she sat on the first pew and surveyed her work. The musty smell had been replaced by the scent of cleaner, but the wooden cross hanging on the wall in front of the room was still dull and needed to be dusted.

"Cassie?"

She jumped, her heart sticking to the back of her throat. She turned around to see Pastor George standing in the doorway clutching a Bible.

She hurried to his side. "What are you doing here?"

Pastor George had celebrated his eighty-fifth birthday a month earlier. He was the pastor at the church she had attended since she started working at the canyon. His thin white hair was combed back perfectly, and he wore his usual non-Sunday outfit—tan polyester pants and a short-sleeved button-up shirt.

She took his hand. "How did you know I was here in the chapel?"

They sat together on the nearest bench. "I didn't. When I couldn't find you in your office, I thought I would spend some time here in prayer. I love the windows."

The little chapel was much different than their church in the country. Their church had a small sanctuary and three Sunday school rooms through a small door in the back. Members sat on folding chairs, the windows were small and clear, and the walls were white. On many Sundays, the entire congregation could have fit into the chapel.

Most members of the church were much closer to Pastor George's age than her own. The closest person to her in years—other than Beth—was a man in his forties who lived in a trailer with his ailing mother.

"Thank you for coming out to visit me, but you know I would have come to you if you had called me."

Pastor George's eyes were the bluest eyes Cassie had ever seen. Barbara, who played the piano for the three-person choir, had once told her they got brighter every year.

"I haven't been down here in almost a year. I wanted to see it," he spoke slowly. "You may not know this, but I met my late wife, Susan, here when I was seventeen and she was fifteen."

"You never told me that."

He folded his hands over his Bible. "She was from a couple towns over. The town doesn't even exist anymore, but I knew the second I saw her that God meant for us to be together."

Cassie propped her elbow on the back of the pew and rested her head on her hand. "And you were together from that day on?"

Pastor George closed his eyes when he laughed. "Child, I said I knew in that moment. God didn't let her in on the secret until many years later after she graduated from college."

"God sure takes His time sometimes," Cassie said.

He nodded. "But He always has a good reason for it, whether or not we understand it."

Pastor George moved over where the yellow light coming through the window could shine on his face. "Cassie, I have another reason for coming to see you today."

She sat straighter.

Pastor George placed his cool hand on hers. "I'm having surgery tomorrow."

Cassie's stomach tightened.

He patted her hand. "Now don't worry."

She couldn't bear to think of anything happening to Pastor George. She had never expected him to become like family. Maybe it was because he reminded her of her own grandfather, solid and dependable.

"It's not serious, but I won't be at the church to deliver the sermon on Sunday."

Cassie loved Pastor George's sermons. He preached straight from the Bible. He could make an Old Testament story she had known since she was a teenager feel new again. "I don't understand," Cassie said. "Someone is going to fill in until you recover?"

Pastor George's eyes were moist. "It's time, Cassie. It's time for us to close the doors of the church so God can do new things."

Cassie locked her hands together to keep them from trembling. "But I love our church."

"This has been trying for me, too, but God will provide for you."

"I don't want to find another church," she whispered.

"It's time," he repeated, patting her arm.

He moved to the front of the chapel, and she helped him into one of the pews. When he bowed his head to pray, she needed to escape from the hot air and the walls that were closing in on her. The thought of losing her home church as she faced losing the camp she loved was too much for Cassie to bear.

&

From the moment Will saw Cassie plodding down the gravel drive, he knew something had upset her. He pulled the silver sports car up beside her and rolled down the window.

Streaks of tears ran down Cassie's face. He jerked the car into PARK and climbed out of the car as fast as he could. "Cassie, what's wrong?"

She looked away from him and rubbed both hands across her cheeks. "I'm fine. It's nothing."

He ducked down where he could see her face. "You're not fine. What happened?"

She laughed nervously. "It's no big deal. Just some disappointing news."

Will waited for more.

Hesitantly, Cassie said, "Pastor George is having surgery. I'm worried about him, and it looks like our little church will be closing. Must sound like a silly thing to cry about."

Will hadn't realized the little country church was still meeting. He reached out and squeezed her shoulder. "It's not silly at all."

Cassie fanned her face with her hands, drying her wet cheeks. "What are you still doing here?"

Will could see the pain through her forced smile. He wanted to fix it, but if she didn't want to talk about it anymore, he wouldn't try to force her. "Actually, I was looking for you."

Cassie shifted her weight from one leg to the other. "Oh. . . okay."

Will considered his words. Before he met with his father, he needed to find out if Cassie would even be open to what he had in mind. "I wanted to tell you that if you ever need any advice on the business side of the camp that I would love to help."

Cassie pushed back a strand of hair that blew across her eyes. "What do you mean?"

"I've heard this place is struggling, and I have a lot of experience in the real-estate business, and this is a real-estate problem, more or less."

Her slumped shoulders straightened. "Who told you the camp was struggling?"

It was pretty much common knowledge around Wyatt Bend. Surely she knew that. "I guess I shouldn't have said 'struggling.' I heard finances are tight. I'm just offering to help you."

"How could *you* help?" Cassie asked.

It sounded more like a challenge than a question. "I could

take a look at the finances. We could go over the business plan."

In an instant, the vulnerable woman he had just witnessed had rebuilt the walls around herself. "Thank you," she said through her clenched jaw. "But I don't need any help. I do perfectly fine here on my own."

seven

When Beth pulled the car up to the pink brick building with large glass doors, Cassie pursed her lips in an attempt to hide the dread. She could think of a million reasons to ask Beth to turn around and skip church altogether.

Cassie's church was closed, she still had a lot to do before Mr. Hartley arrived, and she could use a day to relax after a crazy week of campers. Somehow she had managed to get out of bed and put on a cotton dress and sandals before Beth had arrived.

"Tell me again why you chose this church," Cassie said.

Beth had been attending Pastor George's church with Cassie. When they were left without a service to attend, Cassie asked Beth to choose the church they would try. She never thought Beth would pick out the one Will attended. A couple of days ago, Cassie had been relieved that Will was out of her life for good. She hoped to keep it that way.

"Well, a lot of people love it here," Beth said. "And it's the biggest church in town. You shouldn't have any trouble avoiding Will if he's here."

The only experience Cassie had with a larger congregation had been in high school, and it hadn't been a positive one. The girls in the Sunday school class hadn't accepted the new girl full of questions. She had always felt safer in a tiny church. Cassie took a deep breath, trying to calm her nerves.

They made their way into a sanctuary ten times larger than what she was used to. The twenty choir members wore robes, and the sound system was nicer than the one she had in the

61

tabernacle. They found seats on the back row. Cassie opened the glossy bulletin. The first announcement on the page was for the upcoming men's retreat at Sunset Camp. Cassie made a mental note to check on all the details for the retreat when she returned to the office. It hadn't occurred to her until now that Will might be part of the retreat. Suddenly feeling warm, she fanned herself with the bulletin.

When the music started, she couldn't deny that the voices of all those people singing a hymn together moved her. She loved and missed the distinct voices of her old church, but this was beautiful in a different way. Strong and powerful, the notes and words seeped into every pore.

The words to the hymn caught in her throat when she saw Will near the front of the sanctuary singing with his eyes closed. What was she doing here?

Cassie gripped the hymnal more tightly. Will knew the camp was struggling, and he had asked to know more. She wished that she could believe he wanted to help, but he wouldn't gain anything by helping her. She understood how business worked.

When the service concluded, Cassie didn't linger in the church but headed to the parking lot. She didn't want to risk running into Will.

She stopped outside the front door to give Beth a chance to catch up to her.

"That wasn't so bad, was it?" Beth asked as she walked up beside her.

"It was nice," Cassie said, and she meant it.

Beth touched her arm and gestured toward something with her eyes. Cassie looked over to see Will coming toward them.

She looked to Beth for help, but it was too late to escape. Beth simply shrugged her shoulders. "I'll be in the car if you need me."

Will looked different without the gym shorts and T-shirt. Today he was striking in a gray suit and white shirt, like someone right off the red carpet. "If I didn't know better, I would think you were trying to get away from me," he said to Cassie.

Cassie fidgeted with the tips of her fingers. "Hi, Will."

"I'm sorry about your church, but I'm glad you're here."

"Thanks," she said.

An awkward silence hung between them. Will pulled at the collar of his shirt. "I wanted to talk to you about the men's retreat."

Cassie should have known this was coming.

"You've been working with Craig, right?" he asked.

Cassie nodded.

"Craig's pregnant wife is on bed rest. I volunteered to take over the planning while he takes care of his family stuff."

"I hope everything is okay," Cassie said. "If you talk to him, let him know they're in my prayers."

A tall man in a cowboy hat patted Will on the back. Will shook his hand and watched as the man walked away. "He'll appreciate that. I'm not sure what needs to be finalized before the retreat."

Cassie bit the inside of her lip. She hated dealing with all the insecurities and fears about his motives. Now she would have to add Will back to the list of stresses in her life. "You can call next week," she said in her most professional voice. "We'll iron out all the details."

He stared at her as if he wanted more, like she hadn't said what he wanted to hear. "Okay then," he said. "I guess I'll be in touch with you."

She turned to leave.

"Cassie, wait."

Cassie pivoted around.

He held his open hands out toward her. "I also wanted to apologize about the other day. I didn't mean to offend you or insinuate that you're not great at what you do."

She nodded. "I appreciate that." She turned and walked toward the car. She could feel him watching her.

Beth was waiting for her with the motor running. "What was that all about?"

"Just business," she said.

⁓

Will flipped through the schedule on the receptionist's desk. *"9:00 a.m. Marvin Hartley."*

It was written in his father's handwriting. "Dad," he yelled down the hallway. Will carried the spiral-bound book to his father's corner office. "Did you schedule a meeting for me this morning?"

"Yes." His dad swiveled his chair from his file cabinet. Their offices on the Wyatt Bend town square weren't fancy, but the old building certainly had character, with original hardwood floors and exposed brick walls like the one behind his dad's desk.

"I'm having a meeting and thought it might be good for you to come along," his dad said.

His whole life, people in town told Will he looked like a younger version of his father. Will used to deny it, but every now and then his reflection in the mirror would catch him off guard. If his dark wavy hair turned gray and he had a few more laugh lines, they might be difficult to tell apart. "Okay, but who is Marvin Hartley?"

His dad rested his elbows on a pile of plat maps and blueprints on his desk. "I can see you haven't done your research. Marvin is the director of camps for his denomination's conference. He runs the board that makes all the decisions regarding Sunset Camp."

Will's muscles tightened. His lack of progress toward purchasing the camp was already causing his dad to lose faith in him. "Dad, I've already explained to you that I need more time."

His father stood and walked around the old oak desk. "It's simple. If we don't step in soon, another investor will."

Will dropped the schedule on the wingback chair. "You always tell me that I need to learn to trust my gut."

His father raised a gray eyebrow. "Connor mentioned you met the camp director while you were there."

His brother had a big mouth. "Of course I met her."

"She wouldn't have anything to do with your resistance to this deal, would she?"

Will looked out the window toward the courthouse. "You don't give me enough credit."

"Then why would we hold back?"

Will turned to face his father. "I think I could help them. I'd hate to see that place close if it didn't have to. It just doesn't feel right."

His father sat on the edge of the desk. "Son, I appreciate where your heart is, but don't be naive. The camp is in serious financial trouble. Either we're going to purchase it or someone else will. We could make something great out of that place. Imagine how much business the extra tourism will bring to Wyatt Bend."

Would he really be doing it for Wyatt Bend, or would he be doing it for his father? Would he be doing it for the money?

His dad walked to Will and slapped him on the back. "Come on, son. We're meeting Marvin Hartley for coffee. It won't hurt to talk to the man."

Will clenched his jaw. Cassie probably wouldn't see it the same way.

By Monday the camp looked better than Cassie had ever remembered seeing it. All her staff had agreed to come in on Sunday to clean and make repairs. Emory had planted flowers around the sign at the entry of the camp, and Beth baked, filling the cafeteria with the sweet smell of cookies and bread.

Still, Cassie's stomach twisted into a knot. She hadn't slept the night before, unable to turn off the thoughts running through her mind. She felt like Mr. Hartley was coming to judge not only how well she was running the camp, but how well she was running her life, which hadn't been going so well.

Mr. Hartley had called on Friday and bumped their meeting time back by two hours. A last-minute change was unlike him, but so many things surprised her these days.

She sat in her office going over the books one more time in case he had questions about the finances. She had a list of things she wanted to tell him, things she had done to improve the camp and plans she had for the future of the camp. Beth had even been by to wish her luck.

She watched as Mr. Hartley's white Lincoln pulled in front of the cafeteria. She walked outside to meet him. He wore his usual khakis that were a little too short and a shirt that fit a little too tight. He had never been anything but kind to Cassie, but he had also never been afraid to speak the truth to her. When he first let her take the job as director temporarily, he spoke of his concerns about her openly, especially the fact that she was the youngest person ever to run one of the camps in the state.

"How are you, Cassie?" he asked in a straight, monotone voice.

"Fine, Mr. Hartley. How was your trip?"

He took an old, battered briefcase out of the backseat of

his car. "There were too many trucks on the highway."

Cassie clasped her hands together. "Well, what should we do first? Would you like to take a quick tour around the grounds?"

He nodded. "That would be fine."

They walked through the common area to the tabernacle, down the gravel road past the snack bar and swimming pool, and by the small-group areas. Cassie pointed out the new signs around the pool and the potholes in the road that they had filled. She took him into the cabins that had been renovated, including cabin five with the new mattresses.

He didn't say much, keeping quiet except for asking an occasional question like how many campers they had had during the summer and whether they had any problems with the wildlife this year. He wrote the answers in a small notepad he had removed from his shirt pocket. He snapped the pad shut when she tried to peek at what he had written.

She bit the inside of her cheek to keep herself from blabbering to fill the silence.

"Did you have any problems at the camp last week?" he asked.

"Not really," she said. "We had a bit of a prank war, but nothing serious."

"What do you mean?" he said as he looked at the playground one of the local churches had installed as a project. He wrote something in his notebook.

"Pink dye in the swimming pool," she explained.

He pushed his glasses up on his nose.

"Just teenagers being teenagers," she said.

He clicked his pen and flipped the little notebook to a new page. "And were there others?"

She was tempted to take the little notebook and throw it into the swimming pool. "It was no big deal."

He stared at her.

There was no graceful way to describe it. "Boxer shorts strung up the flagpole."

Instead of the humor defusing the tension, Mr. Hartley's lips formed a thin line. "Let's head back to the cafeteria," he said.

In the cafeteria, she offered him the oatmeal cookies Beth had baked, but he politely declined. Beth would be disappointed. He asked that they go somewhere to talk, and she led him into her office. Her foot twitched as he dug through his briefcase, overfilled with papers and folders. She mentally prepared herself for the dreaded news: him telling her they found a new director or, worse, that they were shutting down the camp.

She studied his face to figure out exactly why he was there, but it held no expression. Finally, when she couldn't stand the suspense, she took a deep breath and asked, "Mr. Hartley, why did you come today?"

He looked up at her with wide eyes and his mouth slightly open.

"I don't mean any disrespect to you," she continued. "You have the right to come here whenever you please, but it was so unexpected, and you didn't tell me much in the e-mail." She was rambling now and resolved to let him answer.

He wiped his brow before opening a folder and handing her a sheet of paper. "You deserve to know why I'm here."

Her eyes scanned the words, trying to make sense of them. It was the itinerary for the next board meeting, but it didn't give her any explanation as to why Mr. Hartley was in the camp. She looked up at him.

He reached over and pointed at the page. "Look at item number six."

She read down the page until she saw number six. It simply read, "Sunset Camp."

"They're going to talk about us at the board meeting?"

Mr. Hartley stuffed the piece of paper back in his briefcase. "Cassie, they're going to talk about closing this camp and holding all the camps that meet here at one of our other locations."

Cassie could feel herself getting choked up. She couldn't look at him, so she turned and looked out the window. "We're closing."

"Not yet. It is on the agenda to be discussed. Nothing is happening right away."

His words didn't do anything to ease Cassie's fears, which left her numb.

"But if they vote to close the camp, it will happen this fall," he said. "This has been our least profitable camp for a long time, and now that Henry is gone. . ."

Cassie put her hands on her desk. "But we're trying to change all that. I've come so far working with our books and our finances. I need the rest of the year to get it all straightened out. We would be doing great right now if we didn't have to take care of some things that weren't being done properly for so many years."

Cassie didn't know if her words meant anything to Mr. Hartley or if they would mean anything to the board. Everyone loved Henry Mason. Cassie wasn't trying to speak poorly of the man, but simply state the facts about where the camp stood.

Mr. Hartley pushed his glasses up on the bridge of his nose. "This is why I'm here—to get all the information before the next board meeting. I'll probably be asking you to send me some documentation this week for a presentation I'll put together."

"Is your presentation going to be for or against this camp?" she asked.

"It's not like that, Cassie. I'm just giving them the truth about the camp's status."

Cassie took a deep breath, fighting back the desire to say something she shouldn't while rambling. "I'll do anything I need to do to cooperate."

He pulled the notebook out of his pocket and clicked the end of his pen.

She swallowed hard. "But you should also write down that I'm going to do everything I can to save this camp. It has meant too much to too many people to be closed down because of a financial mess we are making our way out of. I need more time. I can do this."

He nodded but snapped the notebook shut.

eight

Cassie didn't have time to sit and mope about Mr. Hartley's visit, because after he left, vans of new campers poured into the canyon. This was the biggest group they would have all year, and the cabins would fill to capacity. She threw herself into the work, directing campers where to go, helping Beth prepare to cook the first of many large dinners that week, and fielding requests from counselors.

One of the small-group leaders who would be meeting in an outside area had requested an ice chest. Cassie struggled to open the heavy door to the garage where she stored them. The garage also housed hoes, rakes, and hundreds of other odds and ends. Emory kept everything on neat rows of metal shelving.

Cassie poked around until she found an ice chest behind a stack of folding tables. She tried to pull it out, but it was jammed in the space. She jerked it, and the shelf beside her rattled. A large metal flashlight rolled off the top shelf and smashed into her foot. The sharp pain knocked her to her knees, and tears stung her eyes. Because of Mr. Hartley's visit, she had worn leather flats in place of her usual hiking boots.

She tried to stand, but her big toe felt on fire. A whimper escaped her lips.

She pulled herself over to a folding chair beside a Weed Eater and managed to lift herself into the seat. She grimaced as she tried to remove her shoe without it touching the toe. It was already swollen and beginning to bruise. *Why now, with everything at stake?*

71

She tried to stand on her uninjured foot, but even moving was almost unbearable. She fought back the tears as she hopped toward the open garage door.

She made it to the door and leaned on the outside wall to rest. She looked down to see a toe she didn't even recognize. Her toenail looked full of blood. Staring down the gravel road back to camp, she couldn't imagine how she would make it back on one foot without anything to hang on to. She bit her lip, fighting through the pain of her throbbing foot.

Just as she was embarking on the impossible journey to find Beth, the little silver car she had watched leave her camp only a few days earlier turned down her road. She blinked back the tears forming in her eyes. She couldn't let Will see her crying again.

She breathed a sigh of relief when he drove past her, but the car wasn't ten feet beyond the garage when the brake lights shone and the car reversed toward her. Will was out of his car and by her side in seconds.

"Are you okay?" He looked down at her foot and then back to her. "What happened?"

She stared at her foot. "Something fell on my toe. I'll be fine."

He bent down to examine it.

She jerked her foot away from him. "Don't touch it!"

He turned his eyes up to her. "I'm not going to touch it. I promise. Let me look at it."

When she didn't move, he stepped back from where she stood holding her foot. "I think you broke it."

"It's not broken." It couldn't be. Cassie didn't have time for broken bones. "I'm sure it's only bruised."

"Either way, we need to get ice on it," Will said.

Cassie cringed at the word "we." She still didn't want Will's help, and she didn't want him seeing her as the helpless damsel in distress. She steadied herself against the wall and grimaced.

"Do I need to carry you to the car?" Will asked.

Cassie wobbled and caught herself. "I definitely do not need you to carry me anywhere."

She hopped on her good foot toward the car but soon realized she wasn't going to be able to keep her balance when she reached the gravel. She couldn't bring herself to ask him for help. Fortunately, he must have seen the anguish in her eyes. He didn't try to pick her up but wrapped his arm around her waist and put her arm on his shoulder. He was so much taller than her that he had to stoop down for her to hold on to him.

He walked slowly, letting her set the pace. After she steadied herself beside the passenger-side door, he opened it for her and held her hand as she sat. She leaned back in her seat as he ran around the car and slipped into the driver's seat.

She gasped.

"What's wrong?"

"I forgot to get the ice chest," Cassie said.

"I'll wait on you while you hop on in there and get it."

She couldn't help but smile. "Very funny. Do you mind?"

He left the car running as he climbed out of his seat. "I'll be right back."

She waited as it took him several attempts to get the unwieldy ice chest in the trunk of the small car.

When they reached the main part of camp, they crept along in his car because campers were everywhere, walking on the road and playing in the grassy area.

Cassie pointed him down a small road leading behind the building to the back door of the kitchen. She tried to stay away from the area after dark, because a raccoon never failed to jump out of the dumpster and scare her out of her boots. But in the daylight it was probably the only quiet place on the campus.

By the time Will had run around the car, she had opened her own door. He extended his hand to her and helped her hop up the five steps without bugging her to let him carry her, which he could have done in half the time it was taking her.

Beth ran out of the screen door, letting it slam behind her. "Oh no. What happened?"

Cassie couldn't speak and concentrate on getting up the steps without slamming her toe into the concrete. Will answered for her. "I found her like this at the garage. She broke her toe."

Cassie jumped up on the last step. "*Bruised* my toe."

Will mouthed the word "broken" to Beth.

"I saw that," Cassie said.

"Should we take her to the hospital?" Beth asked Will.

"I'm right here, Beth," Cassie said. "And I don't need to go to the hospital. I'm fine."

Beth looked back to Will. "She looks like she's been crying. Was she crying? If so, it's bad."

Maybe she should tell Will about the ratty blanket Beth still slept with at night. "Beth!"

Once inside the kitchen, Will opened the ice maker, and Beth handed him a dish towel. "There isn't much they can do for a broken"—he cleared his throat—"I mean, a bruised toe. Anyway, they'll probably tell you to tape it to the next toe and keep it elevated." He pulled a chair in front of her from the table where the employees ate in the kitchen. He picked her foot up and placed it on his knee. She squirmed but didn't know if it was because of the pain or his touch. The ice burned worse than if he had lit her foot on fire.

"So," Cassie said, trying to take the attention off her injury. "Do you drive around and look for injured women to pick up in your nice car?"

He looked at Beth. "Is she always like this?"

Beth giggled and slipped out of the room.

"If I remember correctly, you told me that we needed to discuss details for the men's retreat."

Cassie smiled at him. "If I remember correctly, I told you to call. You didn't have to waste your time driving down here."

He readjusted the ice on her foot. "Maybe I don't consider it as time wasted."

Cassie's face burned, and she looked down so he wouldn't see her blushing.

After hopping to her office and finalizing the details for the retreat, Cassie insisted on walking with him outside the back door by his car. She almost tripped over the mat outside the door, but he grabbed her and set her back up on one foot.

With a glint in his eye, he said, "Just let me know if you need anything else."

She grinned. "I'm sure I'll be fine."

He winked at her. "I know you will."

❧

Petal met her at the door, meowing for her can of dinner. Cassie's phone rang as she dumped the smelly mess into Petal's bowl. "How do you eat this stuff?" she asked Petal, who was already devouring the meal.

Cassie tucked the phone between her shoulder and her ear. "Hello."

"Cassie, did I wake you?" her mom asked.

Cassie poured herself a glass of water from the pitcher in the refrigerator. "No, Mom. I just came in from work." She didn't mention her toe. Her mother would just worry. "How are you?"

"Concerned about you. I tried to call you a couple of times this week and could never catch you at home."

Cassie tucked the newspaper Beth had given her under her arm. "I've been busy. Our biggest camp all summer arrived today."

"I talked to your sister today," her mom said, ignoring Cassie.

Cassie didn't even know why her mom told her she had talked to her sister, because they talked several times a day, every day. She sat on the worn sectional couch and set the glass and the paper on the coffee table.

"She told me she sent you an e-mail, and you ignored it," her mom said. "Why would you ignore your sister's e-mail?"

Cassie held the phone away from her ear and took a deep breath to calm her nerves. "Like I said, Mom, I've been really busy."

"I understand, but how long does it take to send a message thanking your sister for thinking of you?"

"How are my favorite nieces?" Cassie said, trying to change the subject. Grandchildren were the easy choice.

"They've gotten bigger. If you would take the time to come visit us, you would know."

Cassie gritted her teeth. "I would love to come see them, but the summers are my busy time of year. It's impossible right now."

"Cassie, you have to make priorities in your life—work or family."

Her jaw ached. "Mom, thank you for calling tonight, but I better get to bed. I have a big day tomorrow."

"Hang on, Cassie. I haven't even told you why I called," her mother said. "I have some exciting news."

Cassie skimmed the front page of the newspaper. "Oh?"

"I think you'll really be surprised. Your sister and I both

promised not to tell until now."

Cassie turned the page. "Hmm."

"She wanted to be here when I called, but one of the girls wasn't feeling well. Nothing serious, just an upset stomach, but you know how it is," her mom said.

Cassie opened the grocery-store insert. "Yeah. Of course," she said and made a mental note to pick up some of the cantaloupes that were on sale.

"Cassie? Are you listening to me?" her mom asked.

"Yes, Mom." Cassie took a drink of water.

"Your sister and I are coming to visit you," her mom said with abounding enthusiasm.

As the words resounded in her head, the water stuck in her throat, making her gag and cough.

"Cassie, are you okay?"

She wiped water from the front of her shirt. "You're coming here—to the camp?"

"Melissa and I are both coming."

Cassie could feel her pulse behind her eyes. "When?"

"We're flying in a week from tomorrow. Your wonderful brother-in-law bought the tickets."

Of course he did. Her mom and her sister, here, in the canyon with her. Sharing her house. "Wow," she managed.

"I know. Isn't it exciting? It will be like old times."

The excitement in her mother's voice caught Cassie off guard. The last time the three of them had been together without the distraction of holidays and Melissa's husband and kids had been years ago. She couldn't imagine what they would do. "How long are you going to be here?"

"We'll fly home on Sunday. We'd stay longer, but Melissa can't be away from the girls any longer."

Cassie's to-do list was longer than it had ever been. She counted through the calendar days, remembering everything she would have to get done. Will's retreat. Her family would be there when it began. "But I'll have to work during those days. I don't want you to be bored."

"We thought about it, but we figured there would never be a time when you weren't working. We'll just tag along. We'll figure out what you actually do every day."

A wave of guilt washed over Cassie. Her mom sounded genuinely excited about the trip, and Cassie should feel the same. She loved her family; she really did, but she couldn't escape all the history and bitterness that came with the relationships. She didn't know if she could keep up the pleasantries without all the old hurts spilling out onto her family.

After her father had left them, she wished they had clung together, but instead they fell apart. Her mom worked a lot to support them, which Cassie tried not to take for granted. She appreciated the sacrifices she made, but at the same time she couldn't forget that her mother had checked out emotionally.

Her mom used to tell everyone how much Cassie reminded her of her father, which wasn't a compliment considering her mom spent most days cursing the day she met him. Even when her mom was at home, she wasn't there. Cassie couldn't remember her ever saying she was proud of her. She only pointed out the ways she didn't measure up, saying, "If only you could make better grades. . .start on the basketball team. . . make more friends."

Cassie's sister, Melissa, had reacted by trying to meet all her mother's wishes, and in Cassie's eyes she had. Melissa was never shy about pointing that out to Cassie. When Cassie fought with her mother in high school, Melissa would say, "Why can't you do what she wants?"

Now they were going to be in her house, judging her, critiquing her life, deciding whether or not she was worthy to be a part of their world.

After she hung up the phone, Cassie scooped up Petal, who acted as if being carried wasn't elegant enough for her kind. Petal squirmed, but Cassie stroked her from her ears to her tail, which made Petal twitch violently. "Petal, we're going to have visitors next week. I hope you're ready."

❧

On Wednesday morning, Cassie leaned against the cafeteria wall, out of breath and frustrated with her lack of mobility. With an injured toe, everything took ten times the amount of energy it would have taken before the flashlight incident. She hadn't slept well with her foot propped on pillows, but an injured toe couldn't stop her. She had too much work to do.

Cassie opened one of the giant ovens and peeked inside to see what Beth was cooking. Her nose had been right— cinnamon rolls.

A dish towel snapped against her arm.

"Trying to sneak a roll before breakfast?" Beth asked.

"You caught me," Cassie said. "Hey, thanks for picking up the slack around here yesterday."

Cassie had spent Tuesday afternoon working from her house. She had to escape from any distractions and get through all the paperwork Mr. Hartley had requested for the board meeting. The thought of it made her queasy.

Beth pointed a wooden spoon at her. "You owe me big-time. Yesterday was crazy."

With the number of campers they had, Cassie wasn't surprised. "I will make it up to you one of these days."

"Someone caught small-group room number two on fire," Beth said nonchalantly.

"What!" Cassie shouted. "Why didn't you call me?"

"It wasn't serious. No damage. Apparently the counselors wanted to create a mood during their prayer time, but you can't leave thirteen-year-olds alone with fire and paper very long. They tried to make a bonfire."

Cassie was breaking out in a sweat. "Anything else?"

Beth went over to the walk-in refrigerator. "The health department inspector stopped by."

"Please tell me everything is okay."

Beth came out with two tubs of chopped fresh fruit. "A great report, as always," she said with her shoulders back. "The kitchen was spotless, especially after getting ready for Mr. Hartley's visit."

Cassie gave her a high five. "It sounds like you had a busy day."

Beth smirked as she poured the fruit into a stainless-steel bowl. "There's something else."

Cassie threw her hands up in the air. "Of course."

"Will came by to see you."

Cassie scrunched up her face. "Will? Again? Why?"

Beth's shoulders rose. "You tell me. Why do you think he would be down here again?"

Cassie didn't know. Hadn't they figured everything out for the retreat? Had she forgotten to go over something with him? "I don't have a clue."

Beth turned around and leaned on the sink. "You don't have any idea why he might have come here to see you?" She was playing with her now, turning everything around with a question.

"What?" Cassie said. "What's going on?"

Beth faced the sink and rinsed a spoon off under the water. "He left something for you."

"What?" She was getting tired of the game. "Just tell me what's going on."

"They're in the walk-in," Beth said without turning around from her work.

Cassie pushed a chair out of the way and limped toward the refrigerator. "You're making a handicapped woman walk all the way across the room. This better be good," she called behind her.

Beth didn't answer.

A blast of cold air hit her as she pulled the door open. On a cart in the center of the walk-in was the largest bouquet of wildflowers she had ever seen. Purple, yellow, red, orange—every color of flower she could imagine cascaded out of a clear glass vase. She looked behind her, expecting to see that Beth had followed her, but Cassie was alone.

She stood back from the flowers for a moment, almost afraid to touch the bouquet, wondering why he had done it. She put her face down close to the flowers and breathed in the sweet, floral scent. Even a tomboy like Cassie could appreciate getting flowers from a man, especially wildflowers. How would he have known they were the flowers she loved more than anything? Sure roses, lilies, and orchids were nice, but wildflowers made her heart dance.

She poked through the mass of blossoms to find a card buried deep down in between the flowers. She pulled it out to find it still sealed. Cassie looked over her shoulder at the door, impressed Beth had resisted the temptation to open it.

Cassie left the flowers in the walk-in and limped past Beth to her own office. She fell into her desk chair and stared at the little white envelope for a moment, afraid to open it. She took a silver letter opener and sliced the top of the tiny envelope with her name written across the front of it in a man's handwriting.

She pulled the plain white card out of the envelope.

These reminded me of you. I hope they brighten your day.

Her heart beat faster. She turned the card upside down on her desk and covered it with her palm then picked it up and read it again.

Beth finally appeared in the doorway with the bouquet of flowers in her arms. "Okay, I didn't want to ask. I promised myself I wouldn't, but I have to know. It's killing me."

Cassie hesitated and then held the card out to her. Beth snatched it from her fingers and held it up to her face. After reading the message, she waved the card in the air. "This guy knows you."

Cassie shook her head. "What are you talking about? A little over a week ago, I'd never even heard of him." And on the day she met Will, she had promised herself she wouldn't fall for his charm.

"I don't know, but the wildflowers, the note. It looks like he has you pegged."

Cassie crossed her arms across her chest. "Please."

"I know. You hate it, but come on."

Cassie shook her head. "He's one of *those* guys."

"One of *those* guys?" Beth asked as she rearranged some of the stems.

Cassie leaned out of her chair and took the card back from Beth. "Yeah. One of those guys who can smooth talk people, but here's the thing. . ."

Beth cocked her head, already acting unconvinced.

"I'm not one of those girls who fall for it," Cassie said.

Beth pointed a finger at Cassie's face. "Then why are you smiling right now?"

Desperate to change the subject, Cassie turned to face her calendar. "My mom and sister are coming to visit next week."

"Well, there went that smile," Beth said, pulling something out of her apron pocket. "I guess you're not happy about this little family reunion?"

"You haven't met my mother or my sister. They're so. . ." Cassie stopped and watched Beth, who was unwrapping what appeared to be a candy bar. "What is that?"

Beth bit off a third of the bar. "It's a Snickers," she said with a mouthful of chocolate.

Cassie put the tips of her fingers together. "I'm assuming that Snickers isn't some new form of health food."

Beth swallowed and stuck her bottom lip out like a four-year-old who had been scolded for not eating her brussel sprouts. "I quit. I hadn't lost a single pound," she said.

"Although I don't condone this new sugar diet, I can't say I'm sad the old one is over."

Beth took another bite. "Really?" she asked with a mouth full of gooey candy.

"Of course. I mean, here I am with no curves, not much of a chest, no rear end, and you're trying to get rid of your beautiful curves."

"You're just trying to make me feel better," Beth said.

Beth was statuesque with curves in all the best places. "I'm serious. You're gorgeous how you are. I know a lot of the teenage girls who walk through the cafeteria think, 'She is shaped sort of like me, and she's hot!'"

Beth's face flushed magenta. "I have the best friend ever." She threw the last bite of candy bar in the trash can and leaned in to wrap her arms around Cassie.

"You didn't have to waste perfectly good chocolate," Cassie said. "That's just unwomanly."

&

For the rest of the day, Cassie couldn't keep herself from glancing at the enormous flower arrangement. Cassie grinned to herself. She had never been boy crazy or the kind of girl who pined over male attention, but she had to admit it felt pretty good, even if it was from someone she hadn't quite figured out.

Her mood quickly came back down to earth when she opened her e-mail and saw Marvin Hartley's name in the SENDER line. Sending two e-mails in a row, as opposed to phone calls, was extraordinarily rare for Mr. Hartley. The only thing she could guess was that he didn't want to face her in person. Maybe because she was the only female director, he feared she would be more emotional than the others. Maybe he was afraid she would cry if he spoke too harshly with her or delivered bad news. Whatever it was, she didn't like it.

She sucked in a short breath before clicking on his name.

Dear Miss Langley:

We have scheduled the date and time for the next meeting of the board. Because it has been an extended period of time since several of the board members have visited the camp, we've elected to accomplish two tasks by holding the meeting in your facilities. . . .

I hope the date and time work within the camp's schedule. Please contact me to confirm everything and to go over the needs (projector, seating, etc.).

Regards,
Marvin Hartley

The date was sooner than Cassie had expected, less than three weeks away. She wiped her damp palms across the legs of her pants. Not only was she going to face the people who could take the camp away, but she also needed to treat them as distinguished guests in her camp. She cringed thinking about it, and then remorse swept over her. Wouldn't God want her to show them love as He commanded her to show love to anyone whom she came in contact with day to day? The lines between fighting for what she believed to be right and showing kindness to those who threatened to take that away from her were blurry, as they were with Will.

She took one of her Bibles from the shelf above her desk. She flipped to the concordance in the back and ran her finger down the list of topics.

Ambition, anger, anxiety, confidence, forgiveness—so many of them fit. She stared at the word "enemies" but then went back to a word better describing what she needed: courage. She stopped and flipped to the page number beside the word and looked up Deuteronomy 31:6 in her Bible.

"Be strong and courageous. Do not be afraid or terrified because of them, for the Lord your God goes with you; he will never leave you nor forsake you."

Cassie leaned her head back against her chair repeating the phrase "he will never leave you" out loud. She stuck a scrap of paper in the page so she could go back to it later.

What would her own life be like if she hadn't come to the camp? She shivered at the thought. She was ashamed of how she had reacted since she had learned the camp was in jeopardy. She had given up, and the campers were too important to disregard. She couldn't work miracles, but God could.

She moved the mouse on her sleeping computer to change the screen saver of swirling lines back to her e-mail. She clicked the REPLY button and rubbed her hands together.

Dear Mr. Hartley,
*   I would be happy to host the board meeting here at the camp, and the dates and times you sent are available on our schedule. I'm sure we can accommodate whatever needs you might have.*

I do have one request to ask of you. I would like time to speak at the meeting. No one knows this camp better than I do, and I would be grateful for the chance to fight for it.

God bless you,
Cassie Langley

Cassie held her finger on the SEND button, working up enough nerve to press it. She leaned back and closed one eye and hit SEND.

nine

The next morning Cassie attempted to pull the tape off her toes. It felt like she was pulling her toenail off with it, but after several minutes of convincing herself to rip it off, she managed to expose the injury. Her entire toe had turned several shades of black, purple, blue, red, and yellow and was swollen to almost twice its normal size.

Her toenail was the blackest part of her toe, and she had little doubt it wouldn't be there for long. Luckily, people didn't see her feet very often, but she still hoped a new toenail would eventually take its place.

When Cassie arrived at her office, the sweet smell of the bouquet that welcomed her. She straightened the vase on her desk. She needed to thank Will, but she didn't know what to say to him.

Forcing herself not to think about it, she dialed the number written in her schedule on the first day of the men's retreat.

"Overman Real Estate," said a woman with a perky voice.

Cassie tapped her ink pen against her forehead. "Um, yes." She stalled, trying to remember what it was she wanted to say. "Is Will available?"

"No, I'm sorry. He's out of the office right now. Can I take a message?"

The tension drained from her shoulders. Leaving a message was the easiest thing to do. "Please tell him Cassie called to say thank you."

"Okay," she said, sounding a little confused. "Will he know what it's regarding?"

"Why don't you tell me yourself?" Will said from the doorway.

Cassie sat with her mouth open, not knowing what to say. This guy was persistent.

"Ma'am? Are you there?" the woman on the phone said.

"Yes. Um, sorry. You can disregard the message."

By the time she had placed the phone back in the receiver, Will held the silver frame with a photograph of Cassie's family.

Will's dimples appeared on his cheeks. "These have to be your relatives."

Cassie took the frame. In the picture she stood beside her mom, with her sister on the other side of her. Their oval faces and small features stared back at her. Cassie's were even more pronounced with her hair pulled off her face. "I guess we do look alike."

He took the frame and set it back on the desk. "So, it sounds like you spoke with Lillian."

Cassie grinned. "Your sister?"

Will nodded.

"I was calling to thank you for the flowers. They're beautiful."

"I'm glad you liked them," he said.

She narrowed her eyes. "I don't want to sound ungrateful, but what are you doing here?"

He leaned on the doorframe. "I came to check on you and see how you're doing. I was worried about you."

There he went again with his unending need to help her, but this time it was sweet. "I'm—"

"Fine. I know. You don't need me checking on you, but I enjoy it."

He didn't wear a suit jacket as he had at church, just slacks and a crisp, white shirt. Some kind of fancy cell phone device was clipped to his brown leather belt, and a big silver watch hung between his hand and shirt cuff. "Sometimes I need an excuse to escape work."

She tapped the ends of her fingers on her desk. "So, you have a different injured woman who you visit every week. Gives new meaning to *ambulance chaser*."

His eyebrows rose. "No, but you're funny."

When he sat, she had to move the vase to see his face clearly. "What's going on at work—family problems or business problems?"

"I didn't say there were problems, just that I wanted to get away."

She wiggled her finger toward his phone. "Your gizmo there is flashing."

He didn't look down at it, but Cassie couldn't help being distracted by it. "Aren't you going to answer it or take it back to the dealership or something?"

Will hit a button, turning off the device. "Truthfully, I can't stand this thing, but my brother thought it would be a good idea if we all got one. Now they can reach me whenever they want, but I'm not sure it's a good thing. Sometimes I just need to escape."

Cassie understood how he felt. Sometimes she needed an escape from her entire life. "You're welcome to hide down here for a while," Cassie said. "But what do you do for fun when you don't have impaired women to keep you company? Do you have hobbies? Or is it all work, all the time? When you're not stalking me, that is."

He picked up a bloom that had fallen on the desk and tossed it toward her. "I can't tell you."

She picked up the flower and stuck it behind her ear. "Why not?"

"Because you would give me a worse time than my family already does."

"Now I'm intrigued. What if I guess it? You'll tell me then, won't you?"

He let his shoulders slump. "I guess."

She tried to picture him playing golf but decided he would be too impatient for golfing, and he wouldn't be embarrassed enough about it not to tell her. When she couldn't think of a hobby that might be possible, she guessed taxidermy more to see a reaction out of him than anything else.

"Taxidermy?" Will asked. "No, of course not. Why would you think that?"

She pretended to consider it a moment longer. "No? Really? I thought I had it."

"What else do you see me doing in my free time?"

"Noodling?" she asked.

"I don't even know what noodling is," Will said.

"Noodling involves trying to catch a catfish by sticking your arm into holes underwater and getting a fish to latch onto your bare hand," she said, reaching her arm out to demonstrate. "And let me say, I meet some interesting people in my job."

He shook his head. "You're a terrible guesser."

She stroked her chin. "Stamp collecting? Knitting? Espionage? Scrapbooking?" She named off everything that popped into her mind.

He held his hands up in the air. "Okay. I give up. Come out to my truck, and I'll show you."

Cassie stood, feeling satisfied she had won and he had given up. She limped from behind her desk.

Will pointed at her foot. "Fine, huh? Looks like you're still in some pain."

"It's not broken," she said.

A broad grin spread across his face. "Uh-huh."

When they walked outside together, she looked for the

little silver car. "Where's your car?" she asked when she didn't see it.

He stopped and looked over his shoulder. "Oh. . .that wasn't my car."

Cassie was confused. He had been driving it both times she had seen him in a vehicle. "It wasn't?"

"My friend was moving. I loaned him my truck, and I drove his car last week."

"Huh."

He looked at her and spun his hand in a circle in front of her face. "What is this?" he asked.

"What?"

"This look you're giving me."

She pretended to be insulted. "I'm not giving you a look."

He snapped his fingers. "You think of me differently depending on if I drive a little sports car or a pickup."

He looked entirely too amused by his new revelation. "I most certainly do not care what you or anyone drives. I'm not that shallow."

"Oh I don't think you're shallow. I think you thought I was a pretty boy."

Cassie crossed her arms. "That's not true."

"Sure," he said, drawing the word out.

"I'm serious. That kind of thing doesn't matter to me."

"What do you drive?" he asked.

Cassie didn't want to answer him. "You haven't told me what your hobby is yet."

"I'm going to show you, but don't try to change the subject. I want to know what you drive."

Cassie could tell by the smirk on his face he wasn't going to let it go. She breathed an overexaggerated sigh. "I drive a truck."

She expected a sarcastic comment or a loud, hearty laugh,

but instead all she got was a quiet, "Ah."

She looked up at him, and he was smiling. He nudged her with his elbow.

They walked down the sidewalk to Cassie's dream truck. She tried not to let on how much she admired his vehicle. She had loved pickups since her grandpa had taught her how to drive his in an empty parking lot when she was fifteen. She wasn't an easy student because she was headstrong, and she liked to drive fast.

He led her around to the truck bed. She looked over the edge to see a miniature airplane taking up most of the bed. It looked like an actual two-seater plane someone shrank in the dryer.

"What is that?" she asked.

"It's an RA aircraft."

"A what?"

He laughed. "A radio-controlled plane."

It didn't look like any remote-control toy she had ever seen her nieces play with at Melissa's. It looked expensive. He had it tied down with rope and bungee cords. "Cool. How does it work?"

He opened the passenger door and picked up a remote larger than a television remote, with knobs and buttons. "Basically, you control everything from this transmitter. I love flying them, but I also like tinkering with them, fixing stuff and adding better parts."

She walked around to the other side of the truck to get a better view.

"Aren't you going to make fun of it?" he asked.

"As much as I like giving you a hard time, this seems really fun."

He held up the remote. "My family thinks it's a ridiculous waste of time and money."

Cassie was actually a little jealous. She wished she had something she loved to do that didn't involve work. "It's a hobby. Aren't hobbies supposed to be fun and pointless?"

He folded his arms on the tailgate. "I don't know. My brother loves to take his boat out on the lake, and my brother-in-law goes fly-fishing."

"Has he ever been noodling?"

Will's brow furrowed. "Not that I know of. I think since I'm the youngest, they think I don't take things seriously."

"Someday you'll have to teach me how it works."

He held an open hand out to her. "Deal."

She put her hand in his, and as they shook on it, Cassie tried to control the butterflies in her stomach. She slipped her hand out of his.

Will glanced at his watch. "I really do need to get back to the office. If they hear I've been out playing all day, I'll never hear the end of it."

"Can you come back tonight around nine o'clock?" Cassie was surprised the words had come out of her mouth without really thinking about it. She stared at him expectantly.

"Sure. Should I ask why first?"

She shook her head. "No, there's something I think you'd enjoy."

She watched him drive out of the canyon. She liked Will, and it scared her.

❧

Cassie needed to go into town before everything closed at five. Sometimes she missed living in a city where she could go to the grocery store at 2 a.m. Now if she needed something after dark that couldn't be found at a gas station, she was out of luck.

The town of Wyatt Bend was made up of one stoplight, a post office, a few churches, and a downtown the chamber of commerce had spent years trying to rejuvenate. Cassie stopped at the bank, an old building on the town square that was a constant hub of activity.

She stood in line behind a farmer with a local co-op hat and green cow manure on the legs of his wranglers. She smiled at a red-headed boy holding up a sucker the teller had given him.

The teller waved Cassie over. The woman looked a little younger than Cassie and wore a sheer shirt with a camisole underneath. Her fingernails were long and painted in a french manicure, and her hair had perfectly placed highlights. Cassie handed her a deposit slip. The teller's long nails clicked against the computer keyboard. She looked up at Cassie. "You're Cassie Langley."

"That's me," she said, flipping through the checks to make sure she had endorsed them correctly.

The girl leaned in close. Her perfume made Cassie's eyes water. "I heard you're dating Will Overman."

Cassie froze. "Excuse me?"

"Meredith," she called to the teller with identical highlights at the other end of the counter. "This is the one she said was dating Will."

Cassie fumbled for the right words, but the shock of the statement made it impossible for her to think straight. "I'm not dating Will," she said. "I'm not dating him," she said, repeating herself to the lady in line behind her who now stood closer to her.

"He is gorgeous," her teller said. "All the girls here call him Will Head-over-Heels Man."

Cassie tapped her short bare nails on the counter as the girl stared at her and waited for her to respond. "Ah, Will Overman. I get it," she said, trying to sound lighthearted.

"When he comes in here, he's always joking around. Isn't he funny?"

"Um, I. . ." She didn't know how to respond. "Can you please write the balance on the receipt?"

"I heard that last year he was engaged to some girl in the city. She dumped him because he worked too much. What kind of girl would dump him?"

Cassie shrugged and looked around to see who else was listening. She was sure this conversation would be the topic of the town gossip all week.

"Is he romantic?" the other teller asked.

Cassie couldn't help but think about the flowers sitting on her desk. "Like I said, we're not dating."

The girl winked at her and said, "Of course not."

Cassie had to fight the urge to jump on the faux marble counter and scream, "I am not dating Will Overman!"

Hopefully, the talk about her and Will meant they gossiped less about the camp's financial troubles. From the moment Cassie had accepted the job, the town hadn't accepted Cassie and openly shared their skepticism of her. She would never be who they wanted her to be. She was an outsider, a mystery. For a town that liked to be able to refer to someone by his nickname from junior high, a girl from another state who only drove into town when it was absolutely necessary was more a threat than an asset. Maybe that's why everyone wanted to link her to Will. That would mean they had figured her out.

The two girls in the bank began whispering before she could escape through the glass doors. She could feel their eyes following her. When she was alone in her truck, all her insecurities brewed in her mind. They were probably saying that Will was far too good looking and successful for a girl like her.

Cassie skipped the stop at the library she'd planned and headed toward the post office so she could get back to the canyon. But as she drove past a storefront on Main Street with a sign in the window that said BEAUTY BY BETTY, she slowed the truck and made a U-turn in the middle of the street to pull into the parking space in front of the shop. Baskets of geraniums hung in front of the windows dressed with white lace curtains.

She pulled the sun visor down to see if it had a mirror on the inside, which to her surprise, it did. She pulled the black plastic clip off the back of her hair and inspected her straight dishwater blond hair in the tiny mirror.

Sometimes she trimmed it herself, but it had never been colored and hadn't been cut by anyone other than herself in years. Through the window, she saw three women. One woman sat in a chair with her head looking like a silver space shuttle. A lady with short, spiky hair stood over her with a paintbrush and small black bowl, and another woman sat in a chair and flipped through a magazine open on her lap.

Cassie looked down at her work clothes—her favorite pair of khaki pants and a purple shirt. She quickly decided her clothes looked too ratty for an afternoon at the hair salon, not that she had ever spent any time in a salon. Just as she had put her truck in REVERSE, she locked eyes with the woman with the magazine who waved to her, motioning her to come inside. Cassie groaned. Now she was stuck. If she didn't go inside, the lady would think she had snubbed her.

The woman dropped her magazine and stood from her chair, waiting for her to come into the store. Cassie opened the truck door slowly. She forced a smile as she walked into the shop.

The lady with the head of thick black hair and the T-shirt emblazoned with multicolored jewels said, "I could tell you were trying to decide whether or not we took walk-ins. Tammy, I told you we needed to get one of those new signs for the front door. Plus, I can spot a head of hair in need of a trim from a mile away."

"It's true," Tammy said. "One time I went up to the city to the state fair with Betty, and we spent most of our day talking to strangers about what hairstyle would best frame their features."

Betty moved a stack of celebrity hair magazines out of the chair. "What's your name, darlin'?" she asked with a thick drawl.

She was tempted to call Betty "honey." "I'm Cassie Langley."

Betty pointed a comb toward her. "The new camp director. I've heard a lot about you."

Cassie didn't dare ask what she had heard.

Tammy looked down at Cassie's tennis shoe, which she had cut open on the end to make room for her swollen and bruised toe. "Those are some unique shoes."

She held out her foot. "I injured my toe."

Betty took her arm and led her to the chair. "Come and get off that foot."

She pulled her fingers through Cassie's hair. "What are we going to do with your hair today? We're having a special on perms."

Cassie looked at herself in the mirror and then at Betty's reflection. "Well, honestly, I came in here thinking about getting highlights, but I don't think I'm ready for that quite yet."

Betty pulled Cassie's long hair out to the sides of her face. "I agree. You already have a fabulous color. I hardly ever see anyone with her natural color come through these doors. I don't even remember what color my hair really is."

"Mine is gray," the lady with the head covered in tinfoil said. "But nobody else needs to know that."

It felt good for Cassie to laugh with the three women. "So what do you think?" Cassie asked Betty.

"It's not going to take a lot to make you look gorgeous. Look at you. You're stunning. Perfect skin. Beautiful features." Betty spun her around in the chair. She gripped both of the armrests. "Let's give you a great cut. We'll leave it long, past your shoulders, but with lots of layers and movement."

Cassie felt the knot in her stomach tighten. "Will I still be able to get it into a ponytail?"

"When I'm finished with you, you won't want to pull it back."

Cassie put her hands over her face. What was she doing here?

"Come on. It's only hair. If you don't like it, it will grow back," she heard the other customer say.

Tammy stood behind Betty's shoulder in the reflection of the mirror. "The boys will fall all over themselves for you."

"I don't know," Cassie said.

Betty pulled her scissors out of a pocket in a black apron tied around her waist. "A haircut can be like a new beginning, starting fresh. A lot of people come to me when they know something big is about to happen in their lives—a new job, a baby, a marriage, a big move."

Cassie closed her eyes. She could feel them all staring at her. "Okay," she said quickly. "You can cut it."

The three other women whooped and hollered as Cassie stroked her long mass of hair. Betty took Cassie's hair away from her hands and pulled it back in a low ponytail. "I think I better turn you away from the mirror for this," Betty said as she turned the chair around and walked to the other side of her.

Tammy and the customer watched as she felt Betty hold the scissors up to her hair.

Cassie suddenly felt sick, like someone was stealing her

security blanket. "Wait. I don't think I can do it."

Betty held her scissors up in the air.

"I'm sorry. I can't cut my hair." Cassie wanted to explain, but she couldn't think of a reasonable explanation to satisfy Betty. She didn't want short hair. No, it wasn't short hair she was afraid of; it was the idea of having different hair. She couldn't bear to think of it changing.

Tammy put her hands on her hips. Cassie could see in their eyes they weren't going to give up easily. "You know, your hair may be long enough for Wigs for Kids."

Cassie had no idea what she was talking about, but she was glad Betty had taken the scissors away from her head. Betty disappeared through a curtain in the back of the tiny shop and came back with a tape measure and extended it from the ponytail holder to the end of her hair.

Cassie didn't have a clue what Betty was doing. Was this what they always did these days before a haircut? The last time Cassie had a haircut, she had been standing in her bathroom with a pair of kitchen scissors.

Betty looked at Tammy and nodded.

"What's going on?"

Betty picked up her scissors, which made Cassie groan. She had told them she wasn't cutting her hair today.

"Wigs for Kids is a program that takes donated hair and makes it into wigs for kids who lost their own because they were sick. We'd have to cut off a little more than we talked about, but you make the call."

Cassie sat straighter in the chair, running her fingers through her long hair one last time.

"So what do you think?" Tammy asked.

"Let's do it," Cassie said with a sigh.

This time the women didn't cheer but gave tight-lipped approving smiles.

Cassie held her breath as she felt the scissors working their way through the hair that had been with her for so long. She kept her eyes focused on one of the dryer chairs in front of her, afraid if she moved Betty would slip and all Cassie's hair would be gone.

When she felt the ponytail fall away from her head, she felt pounds lighter. She shook her head, and the hair she had left swung above her shoulders.

Betty handed her the hair still held together by the rubber band. "How do you feel?" she asked.

Cassie stared at the hair in shock. She reached her fingers to touch where seconds earlier her hair had been, but she touched nothing but air. A squeak escaped her lips.

"Don't panic," Betty said. "It's going to look great."

A new beginning. That's just what Cassie needed today. "Cut it however you want. I trust you."

"Really?"

Cassie nodded.

As Cassie watched hair fall to the floor, she tried to keep her mind off it by watching Tammy pull the tinfoil squares out of the hair of the woman sitting beside her. Cassie tried to ignore all the gossip about people she didn't know. They talked about divorces and people getting fired at work, alcohol problems, and money issues. She resisted the urge to try to see her reflection as Betty worked.

The foil was now gone from the woman's hair, and it was a shade of frosty blond. She fluffed the blond wisps of hair with her fingers. "Tammy, you always know everything going around town. I don't need to read the paper."

Tammy wrapped a strand of hair around a curling iron. "Oh, you know how it is. When some people sit in this chair, they can't help but tell their life stories."

"Wow," Cassie said.

"What?" Betty asked.

Cassie pressed her lips together, wishing she hadn't said anything. "Oh. . .I was thinking about how much power you guys have."

Betty stopped cutting. "What are you talking about? We're hairdressers, honey, not congressmen."

"Yeah, what do you mean?" Tammy asked with a new interest in her voice.

"You know everyone's problems," Cassie said, trying to figure out how to explain what floated around in her mind. "It seems like it could give you a lot of opportunities to do good."

"I can't go around trying to fix people's marriages," Tammy said with an edge in her voice.

Cassie watched a large chunk of her own hair fall to the linoleum floor. "No, but you sure do have an awesome chance to make some people who are hurting happier by just listening. Plus, you get to make them feel better about themselves by fixing their hair."

The women looked at each other and then back at Cassie.

"Besides," Cassie said, "I'm sure you never run out of things to pray about after you leave here every day."

No one spoke for a minute. Cassie worried she had offended Tammy. After a few seconds, Tammy smiled. "You know, she's right."

"Smart girl," Betty said.

After the hair stopped falling, Betty combed mousse through her hair with her fingers and then spent a few minutes blow-drying it.

Tammy stood in front of her, examining the hair on Cassie's head. Cassie couldn't hear a word she was saying because of the blow-dryer in her ear. "It's amazing," she read from Tammy's lips.

Tammy had finished her customer's hair, but the woman with the blond hair didn't leave the chair, obviously waiting to see the finished product.

Betty turned off the dryer and told them she was almost finished. Everyone oohed and aahed about her new look, but Cassie couldn't help but wonder if she had really looked so bad before the change.

"Are you ready?" Betty asked, her enthusiasm written across her face.

Cassie's stomach fluttered as Betty spun her around in the chair.

"What do you think?"

Cassie couldn't open her eyes, and her hands gripped the chair. She couldn't imagine herself looking any different than she had looked for the last ten years. She didn't know if she liked the attention she was getting over it now.

"Come on," Tammy said, putting her hands on Cassie's shoulders. "Open your eyes."

Cassie slid one eye open and saw a woman she didn't recognize in the mirror. She looked like a woman, not the girl who had walked in the door. Her longest layer rested between her chin and her shoulder. It didn't hang off her head into her face like it used to, but now her hair looked bouncy and light. Bangs swept across her forehead, and the ends of the layers flipped out softly. Her hair was shinier than Cassie had ever seen it. "You did an amazing job," she said to Betty, who stood above her beaming.

Driving back to the camp, Cassie couldn't stop touching her hair. She shook her head, surprised at how light it felt. She braced herself for Beth's reaction. When she spotted Beth walking by the swimming pool, Cassie lowered the window. "Do you want a ride?"

Beth walked around to the passenger door without looking

at her and started talking before she even closed the door. "It's cooler out here than it is in my kitchen. When I get everything on in there, it's like an oven. . .literally."

Cassie didn't speak as she drove toward the kitchen and parked in front of the back door.

Beth didn't seem to notice. "Maybe we could ask Emory to pull the fans out of storage, if he hasn't already taken them apart for their parts."

"Sure. I'll ask him to do that," Cassie said.

"I can't stand the heat—" Beth looked at her and stopped. "Your hair!" she screamed.

Cassie put her finger in her ear to stop the ringing.

Beth's eyes opened wide. "When did you do this? Why didn't you tell me? You look so good," she said, her voice going higher with every word.

"Thank you," Cassie said. "I don't know. I drove by this place, and then it all happened so fast."

Beth reached over and touched a strand of hair flipping away from her face. "I can't believe it. You look so different."

"I feel different."

"Don't get me wrong, you looked great before, but wow," Beth said.

Cassie pursed her lips together, but she couldn't stop the grin from spreading through her lips. "Thanks."

Beth tilted her head. "And you know what, you deserve it."

❧

When Will arrived at the camp, the sun had already slipped away behind the ridge of the canyon. He didn't know what he was doing there, but he was excited to spend time with Cassie, who was sitting on the front step of the cafeteria. As he got out of his truck, campers filed out of their cabins with blankets and sleeping bags draped over their arms.

Cassie looked amazing. The soft light of the porch light

reflected off her face, framed by a new, shorter hairdo. He leaned in and hugged her but pulled away when she stiffened. "I love the new look," he said. "You look amazing."

Cassie pushed her bangs from her face. "It was for charity."

He wrinkled his brow but didn't ask her to explain. Whatever it was, it made her even more of a knockout than she already was. He wanted to tell her she looked beautiful, but he knew she would just resist his compliments. "What are we doing tonight anyway?"

Cassie held the blanket up to him, and he took it. "You'll see."

They strolled toward the tabernacle, taking their time as she limped beside him. They walked near a group of boys laughing about their counselor snoring when he slept.

"I have no idea what's going on here," he said.

Cassie smiled at him. "Just trust me."

A clearing in the trees formed an open grassy area between the tabernacle and the chapel. Campers and counselors were lying on blankets staring up at the sky. They clustered in small groups, their blankets lined up in neat rows. He followed and helped as she spread the quilt behind all the kids. Will stretched his long legs out in front of him while Cassie sat cross-legged on the ground beside him.

"This is a tradition," Cassie explained to Will. "Every year the campers get to stay up late and star watch, but there's a twist."

Will didn't take his eyes off her as she spoke.

"Anyway, the dean always puts things in perspective," Cassie said. "And I thought you might enjoy it."

After some time of spreading out sleeping bags and adjusting and readjusting where they sat, a man finally walked out in front of the crowd. Campers began shushing and whispering.

Completely dark now, stars twinkled in a cloudless sky.

Will leaned in close and whispered into Cassie's ear, "Thanks for inviting me." He loved being near her.

They lay on their backs, Will with his arm under his head and Cassie with her hands resting on her stomach.

" 'God made two great lights,' " the man's booming voice announced. " 'The greater light to govern the day and the lesser light to govern the night. He also made the stars,' Genesis 1:16. 'When I consider your heavens, the work of your fingers, the moon and the stars, which you have set in place, what is mankind that you are mindful of them, human beings that you care for them?' Psalm 8:3–4," he continued dramatically. " 'He determines the number of the stars and calls them each by name,' Psalm 147:4."

The man stepped carefully through the bodies. Will looked around to see each one staring up at the clear sky and the same stars Abraham and Moses looked at so many years ago.

"The distance from the Earth to the sun is about 93 million miles." The speaker took long, dramatic pauses between each of the statements. "The nearest star is approximately 4.3 light-years from Earth. A light-year is the distance light travels in a year and is the equivalent to over 5.8 trillion miles. There are 100 billion stars in our galaxy."

Chills ran up Will's back. His God was a great God.

He looked over to Cassie who had her mouth open with a look of amazement on her face. Will took a deep breath for courage, reached out his hand, and clasped her hand in his. He breathed a sigh of relief when she squeezed his hand. He struggled to listen as the pastor continued to talk about how vast and impressive God's creation was. He stared up at the sky with Cassie's hand in his and thanked Him.

Before he knew it, the man was ending his talk with Deuteronomy 4:19–20. " 'And when you look up to the sky and see the sun, the moon and the stars—all the heavenly array—do not be enticed into bowing down to them and worshiping things the LORD your God has apportioned to all the nations under heaven. But as for you, the LORD took you and brought you out of the iron-smelting furnace, out of Egypt, to be the people of his inheritance, as you now are.'"

The campers were completely silent for several minutes. Will took in the fresh air and the stillness of the night. Slowly campers began standing and gathering their blankets and bags.

"That was awesome," Will said, feeling like he had watched an action movie in the theater.

Cassie stretched her arms over her head. "I thought you might like it. It's one of my favorite parts of the summer."

The kids laughed and talked as they cleared out of the area. Will held out his hand to Cassie and pulled her up off the blanket, and when she stood on her feet, Will didn't let go of her hand. Cassie squeezed his and then pulled her hand away to fold the blanket. The disappointment ran through Will's veins.

"Let me drive you up to your house," he said, not wanting the night to end.

She tucked the blanket under her arm. "That would be nice."

As they walked back to his truck, he noticed her lingering a little closer to him. He hoped her hard shell was softening—that she was beginning to trust him.

He opened the door for her, and then he closed it softly behind her. They didn't speak on the short drive to the house.

As Will remembered his meeting with Hartley, guilt crept in and threatened to ruin his night. He needed to tell her the truth, but he didn't want anything to come between them. Knowing would only hurt Cassie. She was finally letting down her defenses with him. Would she ever be able to trust him if she knew the truth?

Will tried to push it out of his thoughts and take in every moment of the evening.

When they pulled up to the house, he jumped out of the truck and ran around to her side and held her hand as she stepped out of the vehicle. "Thanks again for coming," she said.

He ran his fingers through his hair. It was like he didn't know what to do with his hands. Why was he so nervous? He felt sixteen again.

Cassie smiled.

"I. . .um," he said. "I would love to take you to dinner sometime."

Cassie brushed a strand of hair off her face. "That would be nice."

Her answer surprised him. "Great. When?"

Cassie cocked her head to the side. "Let's do it after the men's retreat."

Will didn't want to wait that long, but he would let Cassie make the rules. He leaned down and pulled her into a tight hug. This time she didn't stiffen.

He breathed in the sweet, clean fragrance of her hair. She leaned into him like she belonged there. He clung to her tightly, wanting to remember every heartbeat.

When she loosened her grip, he took a chance, leaned in, and touched his lips to hers.

Without giving her a chance to react, he stepped backward to his truck, staring into those moonlight-filled eyes and doing everything he could not to scare her away.

ten

"We need to talk," Will said.

Marvin Hartley's eyes peered over his plastic-rimmed glasses. "You drove an hour and a half when you could have picked up a phone?"

Trying to change Mr. Hartley's mind on his turf would be difficult, but it was better than doing it over the phone. "This is important."

Mr. Hartley opened his hand in the direction of the metal chair across from his desk. A fluorescent light buzzed and flickered overhead. "Why didn't your father come along on this field trip to my office?"

Will rubbed his hands together and considered his response carefully. "He wasn't available, but he's aware of what I came to discuss."

Mr. Hartley smirked.

When Will told his father what he planned to do, his father made his dissatisfaction clear, but surprisingly he hadn't tried to talk Will out of it. His father either trusted his instincts or aimed to teach him a lesson. Will took a deep breath to quiet his self-doubt. "After considering it, I've come to the conclusion that before we move forward with further talks of closing the camp, I would like to revisit the idea of—"

Before Will could finish his sentence, Mr. Hartley shook his head. "We've been through this, Mr. Overman."

This wasn't going to be easy. Will normally enjoyed these games of mental chess, but a lot hung in the balance, including his relationship with Cassie. "If you bring me in as a consultant, I could help the camp generate more money."

A deep grunt came from the back of Mr. Hartley's throat. "Mr. Overman, we would simply be prolonging it, which would cost the conference more money. Our analysis shows that it will be more profitable to expand another of our camps when Sunset Camp closes."

Will saw an opportunity and pounced on it. "Then I'll work for free. I thought you of all people would want to try anything to save the camp before closing it. If I'm offering to do this for no cost to the conference, how could you turn it down?"

Mr. Hartley's face puffed up like a red balloon ready to pop. "I'm here to do my job. Part of my job description is to make decisions based on the success of all our camps in the state. If it means making a difficult decision to lose one camp, it's what I'll recommend to the board members."

"Closing Sunset Camp isn't good for anyone," Will said.

Mr. Hartley removed his glasses and leaned back in his chair. "Your father seems pretty set on making this deal happen. What's in it for you to keep the camp running?"

Will swallowed. It was a question that kept him awake at night. Was he doing this for the camp, or was he doing this for Cassie? Even if he saved the camp, he didn't know if Cassie would keep her guard down long enough to return his affection. Was it worth the risk of losing his father's respect? "A lot of lives have been changed in that camp, and there are a lot of people who don't want to see it close. Myself included."

Mr. Harley kept his eyes on Will's. "What about Miss Langley?"

"I doubt your staff members want to lose their jobs," Will said. "I believe Miss Langley is very passionate about the camp."

Mr. Hartley straightened a pile of folders on the corner of his desk. "That's another thing I wanted to discuss with you, Mr. Overman. The board has heard rumors about a relationship between the two of you."

Will opened his mouth to defend himself and Cassie, but Mr. Hartley didn't give him the opportunity to speak.

"The camp director and the real-estate investor getting cozy makes them more than a little nervous. Quite frankly, it makes me nervous, particularly because of our past experience."

Cassie would never do what Henry Mason had. Will had recently learned Henry hadn't retired as everyone, even Cassie, believed. The board had fired him when they learned he was letting the camp's finances go down the drain. The investigation found that an investor had agreed to cut Henry in on the deal if he helped give the board a reason to close the camp and sell the property. Now Cassie was left to clean up the mess, and she had done a pretty good job of it.

And Will was trapped in the middle of it all. He rubbed his hand across his chin. "That's unfair. You shouldn't base anything on hearsay."

"You're right, but your trip here today leads me to believe it could be true," Mr. Hartley said. "With the alleged relationship with Miss Langley and the differing opinions between you and your father, I may need to seek out other investors. I would like to keep things as uncomplicated as possible."

Mr. Hartley had stolen Will's only bargaining tool. He had planned to threaten to walk away if it came to that, but Mr. Hartley had beaten him to the punch. Normally he would have called it a bluff, but Mr. Hartley didn't work that way. He meant what he said, and he could tell from the inflection in his voice that no amount of persuading would change things. Will had done enough bargaining and negotiating in his business to know when he had lost.

Will stood, pulling the cuff of his dress shirt over his watch. "Well, thank you for your time."

"And Mr. Overman," Mr. Hartley said. "If I were you, I'd stay away from Miss Langley and the camp until everything is finalized. We don't want any more of those rumors going around."

eleven

On Saturday morning Cassie and Beth stood in line at Donna's Donuts. Cassie's mouth watered at the sugary smell.

"Did I see Will Overman's truck at camp a couple of nights ago?" Beth asked, like she had caught Cassie in a massive conspiracy.

Cassie stared at the back of a cowboy hat on the man in front of her and struggled to keep the smile from spreading too far across her face. "You did."

Beth gasped. "And? Aren't you going to tell me about it?"

Cassie pretended to read the menu written on a chalkboard hanging behind the counter. "I invited him to come for the star talk."

"You invited him?" Beth's voice moved up an octave. "Don't you know the rules?"

"What rules?" Cassie said, humoring her.

They stepped up a place in line. "You know, let him make the first. Play hard to get. Let him feel like he's in control."

"Ah, those rules." Cassie looked at Beth. "Apparently he didn't mind."

Beth's mouth dropped open. "Why? What happened?"

Cassie laughed, remembering how nervous the normally calm and smooth Will had been before asking her out. "He asked me out to dinner."

"You're going on a date with him?" Beth twisted her mouth to the side. "I mean, he's good looking and successful, but what about the whole real-estate thing?"

Cassie had surprised herself with her change of heart. "I think I underestimated him. I think he's a good guy."

"You don't think he was spying?" Beth asked. "That he wants to take over the camp?"

They walked to the counter. "Let's just say that I'm willing to give him a chance."

Beth's face softened. "Then I'm really happy for you. But be careful. It's the cute ones who will break your heart."

That's what Cassie was afraid of, but right now she didn't care. She felt like a giddy teenager. She crouched in front of the glass case with glazed donuts, bear claws, and apple fritters.

"Go ahead," Beth said. "Get one. It won't bother me."

Cassie stood. "Just a coffee for me, please."

"Make that two," Beth said to the lady with the messy hair piled on top of her head.

Cassie leaned in close to Beth's ear. "Remind me again why you chose a donut shop when you're on another diet."

"They have the best coffee in town—except for my coffee, of course," Beth whispered.

"And I need coffee right now."

Beth elbowed her. "Why? Were you up all night thinking about a certain someone?"

The woman handed them each a Styrofoam cup of coffee. Cassie shook a paper packet, ripped off the top, and poured the sugar into her coffee. "Only if that certain someone you're referring to is Mr. Hartley."

"That's not exactly who I had in mind," Beth said.

Cassie handed the woman a five-dollar bill. "I'm just getting nervous about the meeting. I have a lot to do."

Beth blew steam from the top of her cup. "You've been working your tail off. Mr. Hartley will see that things are turning around."

The woman smiled and nodded as Cassie dropped the change in the mason jar with a piece of paper that read TIPS taped to the outside of it. "Are you girls talking about Marvin Hartley?" the cashier asked.

Cassie and Beth looked at each other. "Yes," they said in unison.

Cassie asked, "Do you know him?"

The waitress tucked an ink pen in her hair. "No. I mean, not really. He was here earlier this week. Tried to pay me with a credit card. Had to tell him I don't trust those little pieces of plastic, especially for a two-dollar ticket."

Cassie's chest tightened. "Mr. Hartley was here?"

Beth put a hand on Cassie's shoulder. "He probably stopped through when he was visiting the camp. No big deal."

Cassie stared at the glass door of the refrigerated case. "I don't know." The donut shop was small and out of the way. "I guess."

Cassie picked up her coffee with a shaky hand and turned to leave.

"Oh, and that man, he was with the Overmans," the woman said.

The words jarred Cassie, and scorching coffee sloshed on her hand. *The Overmans and Marvin Hartley together?* Cassie's empty stomach felt sick.

The woman walked around the counter. "Oh my." She took Cassie's coffee and handed her a handful of napkins from the counter.

"Will didn't say anything to you about it?" Beth asked.

Cassie held her breath and shook her head. She couldn't speak.

"Maybe it wasn't him," Beth said, looking hopeful.

The cashier used a napkin to wipe coffee from Cassie's arm. "From the look on your face, I think I said too much."

Cassie straightened and tried to compose herself to find out more. "No, it's fine. I just didn't know they knew each other. Which of the Overmans were with him?"

The woman looked up at the ceiling tiles. "It was Leonard and one of his boys. The youngest, I think. Will?"

Cassie's fists tightened, and her fingernails dug into her palms.

twelve

When Cassie opened her front door, the vase of flowers on her coffee table mocked her. She carried them to the kitchen, poured the water into the sink, and dumped the flowers into the trash can. As she turned to walk away, the envelope lying on top of the dripping stems caught her eye. She stared at it for a second before she reached in and grabbed it. She flipped it around in between her fingers and slipped it in her pocket.

Cassie marched into the bathroom. She dug the scrubbing soap and a sponge from underneath the sink and pulled a pair of long yellow gloves over her hands. Long hours working didn't give her much time at home, and when she was home, the last thing she wanted to do was scrub the shower or the toilet. If her mom and sister saw her home in the state it was in, they would probably call the authorities. It definitely was not up to their high standards.

The news of Will's meeting with Mr. Hartley had left a blanket of numbness hanging over her. Now she felt the fog lifting. The resentment and feelings of betrayal bubbled to the surface. Sulking wouldn't get her anywhere. She needed to move.

She squirted cleaner in the bathtub. On her knees, she scrubbed the porcelain with all the muscle she could muster. When she thought about Will, she moved faster, scouring every inch of the tub.

Before she could prevent it, tears rolled down her cheeks. She didn't stop to wipe them away. She cried because Will had kept something from her. She cried because she could feel the camp slipping through her fingers, and there was nothing she could do to stop it. She cried because her family was coming to visit, and she already felt inadequate even without their help.

By the time her tears stopped, the tub and toilet sparkled. The spotless mirror reflected her puffy face, red eyes, and the new hairstyle that had promised the making of a new Cassie. But right now it looked like the new Cassie was going to be alone and unemployed.

At the end of the day, Cassie's home was cleaner than she had ever seen it. She stood in the small kitchen and surveyed what she had accomplished. Her stove top gleamed, there wasn't a crumb to be found, and the floor shone. Petal rubbed against her leg.

She expected all the exhausting work to make her feel better, but her chest still ached. Why did everything have to go from good to horrible? Why was God letting her walk through this? She wished Will had never come into her camp.

Cassie turned on the faucet and splashed cold water onto her face. She couldn't get the image of Will and his dad out of her mind. They had probably laughed about how naive and stupid she had been. They were probably relieved when someone so dense was given the task of leading the camp.

When she awoke the next morning, she was still wearing the robe she had slipped on after her bath. She had fallen asleep with wet hair, and now she could feel it sticking out in every direction. The fitted sheet had come off the corners of her bed, and her quilt lay on the floor in a heap.

"Rough night?"

Cassie jumped at the sound of Beth's voice and almost fell off the side of the bed.

"Sorry, but the knocking didn't work," Beth said.

Locking the door had been the last thing on Cassie's mind before falling asleep. She knocked a stack of paperbacks off her nightstand as she reached for her alarm clock. There wasn't enough time to get herself together for church—the perfect excuse not to go. She set the clock down on its side and crawled back toward her pillow.

"I don't think so," Beth said, pulling the sheet off her. Cassie reached for the quilt on the floor without opening her eyes. She was sure she looked like a stubborn thirteen-year-old, but she didn't care. When the quilt wasn't there, she opened one eye.

Beth's tan pointed-toe heel pushed the quilt across the floor out of her reach. Cassie looked up at her. She wore a pleated skirt and a denim blazer. "You look nice," Cassie said weakly.

Beth looked her up and down. "You look. . ." Beth put her fingernail between her teeth. "Tired."

Cassie rubbed the crust out of the edges of her eyes. "Humph."

Beth leaned back to look through the bathroom door. "I see you took yesterday's bad news out on the dirt in your house. Everything looks immaculate."

Cassie swallowed hard. She instantly regretted not brushing her teeth before bed. She pushed herself up and leaned back on the headboard. "The worst part is that I should have known better. You warned me. I knew who he was. Why did I trust him?"

"I guess he's just one of those guys," Beth said.

"You mean one of those guys who can charm anyone? A guy who can get what he wants by virtue of being handsome and charismatic?"

"Yep," Beth said simply. "One of those."

Cassie fell over onto her bed. "I need more sleep."

"No way," Beth said, leaning over to see the alarm clock on the nightstand. "You need to get ready. We're going to be late."

"Not today, Beth."

Beth took her hand and pulled her up from the bed. "Uh-uh. No. You are getting out of bed and coming to church with me."

Cassie crossed her arms. "I really don't feel up to it."

"You need to get out of this house. You can't stay here in your bathrobe all day."

That church was the last place she wanted to be. "Then I'll get dressed and go into the office."

Beth flipped through the clothes in her closet. "I'm not letting you stay here by yourself."

Cassie sat back down. "Then I'll go to a different church."

Beth shoved a khaki skirt into her hands. "Come on, Cassie."

Cassie put her head in her hands. "But what if he's there?"

Beth stopped. "All the more reason to prove he doesn't know what he's up against. You don't have to confront him. Just don't let him do this to you."

"But I—"

Beth cut her off. "Do you want him to think he can make you stay home and cry?" Beth held a white button-up shirt out to her. "It's up to you. Are you going to fight, or are you going to let him get the best of you?"

Cassie had always thought of herself as a tough girl. Why was she letting him do this to her? Before she could change her mind, Cassie took the shirt from Beth.

❧

Will had wanted his parents to meet Cassie at church yesterday, but when he called her name through the crowd, she had only walked away faster.

Will wrestled over what had gone wrong. Their night under the stars had been perfect. How could she act like she didn't even know him now?

He had worked so hard not to scare her away. Unfortunately, Cassie's guarded nature wasn't his biggest worry. He tried to chase away the dread, but the idea that she knew about his meeting with Mr. Hartley lingered in his conscience.

Will walked through the camp, searching for Cassie and the truth about what had happened. He spotted her carrying a bucket from the girls' cabins. A woman with Cassie peered over the edge of the bucket, smiling like a proud mother. Cassie looked naturally beautiful with the top of her hair pulled back off her face.

A girl, whose mouth was dyed green from the Popsicle she held, looked into the bucket and screamed. The rest of the group followed her lead, and it soon sounded like a cute pop star had walked into the camp.

The campers were smaller than they had been the week he had volunteered. He guessed that this was the fifth- and sixth-grade camp he had heard about.

Will walked up behind the group of girls who hadn't noticed his presence and leaned in to see a rat snake coiled in the bottom of the bucket. "Nature project?"

"Who's that?" a girl in braces asked.

Cassie dropped the bucket on the ground, and everyone gasped in unison as it teetered on its end, threatening to dump out the snake. When it stopped safely on the ground, Cassie glared at Will. "What are you doing here?"

"Come on, girls. Let's get back to the cabin," the counselor said as she ushered the girls toward the cabins.

Will studied her face. "I wanted to see you."

"I really don't have time for this right now." Cassie's voice shuddered as she spoke.

This wasn't good. "It won't take long."

She turned to leave. Will reached for her elbow, but she pulled it away. She stopped and stared at him. "I really wish you hadn't come. I don't know what to say to you right now."

Will flexed his hands, trying to calm his nerves. "Why did you run out of church yesterday? I wanted to introduce you to my family."

Her face lost its color. "Will, I don't want to talk about it."

He couldn't leave without answers. "What happened between the last time I saw you and yesterday?"

Cassie looked around them. Then her eyes met his. "I know, Will. I know everything."

The lump in his throat made it hard for him to speak. He stared up at the swallows building nests on the canyon walls. "What are you talking about?" But he knew the answer, and he braced himself for the fallout.

"I know you met with Mr. Hartley."

Will turned around, trying to regain his composure before facing her again. "Cassie, I don't know what you think happened at that meeting, but—"

Cassie wore the hurt all over her face. "Is this why you volunteered to be a counselor? Were you just using the campers to get what you wanted? Because they deserve better than that." With every word she said, the volume in her voice escalated.

"No. I love those kids."

She threw her charges at him like daggers. "Is it why you pretended to like me?"

The words broke Will's heart. Since the moment he met her, he'd wanted to look after her. Now he was the reason for all her pain. "*Pretended* to like you? I didn't pretend anything, Cassie."

Two boys and a leader walking out of the nurse's cabin gawked at them. Cassie moved to the breezeway and opened the door to the nearest small-group room. Will followed. She gripped the back of a chair and leaned in with her head down. "Listen, I'm not as naive as you think."

Will held his hands out open in front of him. "I understand why you would be angry at me, but let me explain."

"What is there to explain?" she asked, her voice trembling. "Did you go behind my back and have a meeting with my boss?"

Will closed his eyes. "I know it looks bad, but my father—"

"Look, I don't want to hear about your father. I can't talk about this anymore. I have to get back to work while there is still a camp." Cassie walked out of the room.

Will ran after her. "Wait. Please, Cassie."

But Cassie didn't stop when he called her name.

thirteen

Work distracted Cassie from the emotions that threatened to send her crawling back to bed. This week's camp was usually one of her favorites. The younger campers made it fun, but because of their ages they couldn't be given much freedom. Everyone on-site had to stay alert, which made the timing of her revelation about Will and her family's visit even more difficult.

She dug through her closet until she found something other than casual work clothes and church dresses. She settled on a denim skirt and a floral top she hadn't worn since her mother had mailed it to her on her birthday. Surely her mom couldn't criticize something she had picked out for her. Petal watched as Cassie forced a leather shoe on her foot for the first time since the flashlight incident.

The shoes weren't unbearable. She could make it through the day with them. She scanned the house one last time, straightening a framed picture on the wall and throwing her bathrobe in the closet. Until now she hadn't noticed the wall in the bedroom needed a fresh coat of paint. She cringed seeing the way her couch sagged in the middle and spying cat hair on the chairs around the dining room table. She needed to leave if she was going to be there when the plane landed.

"Here I go, Petal," she said, holding the doorknob. "Wish me luck."

Petal licked her paw and rubbed it from her ear to her whiskers.

The drive to the city went by faster than Cassie had hoped, not giving her enough time to mentally prepare for her mom and sister. When Cassie arrived at the airport, she joined the small crowd gathered in front of the security checkpoint. A woman fed three kids animal crackers, keeping them quiet. A man in a button-down shirt and jeans held a bouquet of roses, and an elderly couple sat off to the side with their hands locked together.

She searched the row of television screens for the flight number her mother had read to her over the phone. The flight was on time. Cassie, her mother, and sister would all be together again in minutes, and Cassie wasn't ready for it.

Her confrontation with Will had left her shaken. She was still grasping to regain any piece of control in her life. Instead she would have to endure the roller coaster of her family dynamics.

Passengers with rolling suitcases and duffel bags walked toward the crowd. She stood straighter and combed her fingers through her hair. Those around her hugged weary travelers, and men and women in business suits headed straight for the nearest exit.

Finally, after most of the crowd had cleared, her mother and sister came through the narrow security gates. Her mom gripped the top of the brown leather purse hanging over her shoulder. Her stark bob had been dyed a reddish hue. Her sister, Melissa, looked at her cell phone and leaned over and said something to her mother who nodded sympathetically. Melissa wore jeans and a pale pink shell. Two large pearl earrings hung from her ears and matched the necklace she wore. When she looked up and met Cassie's eyes, Cassie waved.

When they reached her, Cassie leaned in and hugged her mom. Her mother reached around her and patted her shoulder. Melissa grabbed Cassie's elbow and made a kissing sound beside her cheek.

"How was your flight?"

"The man in front of me leaned his seat all the way back, practically in my lap, the entire flight," her mother said. "It was quite rude."

Melissa dug through her designer purse covered in little logo letters. "I'll be right back. I need to call and tell Daniel that we made it and make sure he remembered to give Gracie her pills."

She walked away from them, already punching buttons on her phone.

"Is Gracie sick?" Cassie asked her mother. She had been shocked when her mom had told her Melissa was even leaving her daughters behind for nearly a week, but she couldn't imagine her getting on a plane when one of them was actually sick.

"No, she's talking about vitamins. She has her on a strict regimen of natural supplements. They only eat organic now. I've looked into it myself, but it's so expensive."

Cassie watched Melissa talking on the phone with one finger pressed into her ear. "I guess Daniel is doing pretty well then."

Her mother's face beamed. "Oh yes. The first promotion gave him a big raise, and he may get another soon."

If only Cassie had a success to share about her own job, but right now everything was pretty much falling apart.

"I see you cut your hair," her mother said with raised eyebrows.

Cassie pulled at the ends of her hair. "Thanks for noticing. What do you think?"

"Melissa has a wonderful hairdresser. If you ever come out to see us, you should try him. He's pricey, but I think he's worth it."

Cassie felt like the gawky thirteen-year-old whom her mother constantly told to stand up straighter. Melissa rejoined them. "What did I miss?"

"I was telling your sister about Armando," her mother said.

Melissa looked up from her phone. "Armando is amazing."

"Let's go find your luggage," Cassie said.

They followed the signs to an escalator going downstairs, where they joined the group of passengers staring at the empty conveyor belt. The man with the flowers now had a woman on his arm, and the elderly couple chased after a young boy.

"I hope they didn't lose my luggage," Melissa said.

Melissa proceeded to tell Cassie about her playdate friends, her new SUV, and their pediatrician until she reached through the crowd to grab a suitcase with a blue ribbon tied to the handle.

Cassie picked up her mother's old-fashioned hard-backed suitcase. Melissa continued talking about school districts and the latest parenting books as Cassie led them to her truck. Cassie's mother finally cut in. "Cassie, I still can't believe you drive this thing. It's so big and masculine."

Cassie ran her fingers gently down the side of the truck as she walked by it. She adored this truck and would always defend it. "I like it. Plus it's practical for me. We use it a lot at camp hauling tables and different things."

Melissa and her mom gave each other knowing looks, as if confirming they had been right in whatever secret discussions they had about her back home.

The conversation on the drive to the canyon ranged from the curtains in Daniel's new office to the kind of apple juice made with the least processing and preservatives. Cassie's mother talked about the new digital camera Melissa and Daniel had bought her for Mother's Day. Cassie was embarrassed of the gift she had sent—a card and a few books.

"Did you bring the camera with you?" Cassie asked. "You can really take some great photos from the top of the canyon, and I've been thinking about getting a new one. I'd love to test it out with you."

"No," her mother answered, looking out the window. "I didn't think I'd need it here; and besides, I didn't want to mess it up."

Cassie bit the inside of her cheek and adjusted the rearview mirror so she could see Melissa. "We could go hiking tomorrow."

Melissa held her phone in the air and squinted at the screen. She had complained about the spotty reception since they left the city. "I didn't bring any shoes for hiking."

The rest of the drive was quiet. Her sister and mom had never seen the canyon, so when they started driving down the hill toward her home, they looked out their windows. Cassie resisted the urge to justify all the things they saw, like the sign that had broken a few days earlier and the pothole they had already called the commissioner about fixing.

"Doesn't it bother you being so far away from everything else?" her sister asked.

The ridges of the canyon ran like vines through the area. "That's what I love about it. It's peaceful, at least when there aren't a few hundred campers with me."

"And you never think about getting back into the restaurant business?" her mom asked.

Cassie put both hands on the steering wheel. She hadn't considered what she would do if Mr. Hartley shut down the camp. She felt sick to her stomach thinking about it. "I would be happy to be here for a really long time."

"But don't you want something that pays better?" Melissa asked.

The topic of money always came up with Melissa. "That doesn't really matter to me."

Melissa leaned toward the front seat. "Sure it does, Cassie. People say it doesn't matter, but everybody wants to be comfortable and to have nice things."

"But it can't make you happier or more content. I need to do what God wants me to do."

Melissa didn't reply. She always stopped talking when Cassie mentioned God, but it wasn't her reason for saying it.

"Melissa wants you to do everything you're capable of," her mother said.

When they arrived at her home, Cassie lifted her mom's suitcase out of the bed of the truck and carried it up the driveway. "Cassie," her mother yelled, stopping Cassie where she stood. "Are you limping?"

Cassie placed the bag on the concrete.

"She was limping," her mother said to Melissa. "Did you see her?"

Melissa didn't answer.

"What happened? Are you hurt? Why didn't you tell me?" Her mom rattled off the questions.

Cassie hadn't mentioned it to her mom because it should have healed before their visit, and she didn't want her to worry. "I broke my toe, but it's doing much better now."

"Broke your toe?" Her mother looked at her like she had told her she had a second head growing out of her neck. "How?"

"Maybe not broken. Bruised. I was in the storage building, and a flashlight fell on my toe."

Her mom gasped and covered her mouth. "How could a doctor not be able to tell whether or not it's broken?"

"Well, I never actually went to the doctor."

Her mother put her fists on her waist. "Cassie, how could

you not go to the doctor?"

"It wasn't that bad."

"Was someone with you?" her mother asked. "Why didn't they take you to the hospital?"

Cassie took a deep breath. "Someone saw me outside and drove me back to the kitchen, with Beth."

"Who?"

Why had Cassie opened her big mouth? "Who?"

Her mother's eyes narrowed. When she latched on to something, she didn't let it go. "Yes. Who found you and drove you back?"

"One of the counselors."

Her mother didn't flinch. She could sniff out a man in Cassie's life like a tracking dog. Her mom had a gleam in her eye, showing she knew there was more to the story and wasn't letting her get away with not telling her all of it. "A man?"

Cassie looked back to Melissa, who was trying to make a call—again. She considered her answer, finally deciding not to lie. "Yes. He was a male."

She didn't know how her mother knew he wasn't an elderly man or a married man, but somehow she always knew more than Cassie had told her. "Let's get your bags in the house," Cassie said.

This wasn't the last she'd hear from her mom about men, but even so, she was glad her mother had been easy on her for now.

Cassie unlocked the front door and flipped on the light switch.

Her sister came in rolling her bag behind her and holding her cell phone to her ear with her shoulder. "Gracie, you have to brush your teeth for Daddy," she said, almost yelling. "You don't want them to fall out do you?" Melissa nodded her head as she listened to Gracie on the other end. "Sweetie, I know he doesn't sing the 'Brush 'Em' song while you brush your teeth, but maybe you could teach Daddy the song. You can't not brush your teeth the entire time I'm gone."

Melissa looked to Cassie, who pointed her in the direction of the guest bedroom. "Gracie, you're not going to get a prize from Oklahoma if you don't listen to Daddy."

Her mother followed Melissa into the bedroom. "Let me talk to her. Grandma can always get her to brush her teeth."

Cassie went into her own room and sat on her knees in front of her closet. She dug through the pile for the hiking boots that might fit her sister.

Melissa walked into Cassie's bedroom. "Seriously, I don't know how you can find anything in that mess."

Cassie pulled the boots from the corner of the closet and held them up to Melissa. "See. It's actually organized chaos. It just looks like a mess."

Melissa took the boots. She sat on the edge of the bed and held the soles up to the bottom of the sandal she wore.

Cassie stood and pushed the closet door closed with her hip. "I'm so busy keeping everything together in the camp, I don't have much time to organize at home."

Melissa held the boots up to her face and wrinkled her nose at the scuffed toes and the fraying shoelaces. "I know what you mean. It's crazy at my house with the kids. I came in to ask you if I could raid your kitchen. Mom and I didn't have a chance to eat lunch since the flight didn't serve anything."

Cassie smoothed her skirt. "Make yourself at home, but I was thinking we could go down to the kitchen in the camp to eat."

Melissa's eyes narrowed. "Cafeteria food?"

"Beth is a great cook, and I asked her to save us some of the chicken salad on today's menu."

Melissa shrugged like she didn't have the energy to argue

and walked out of the room. Surviving the next few days wouldn't be easy.

"Are you ready, Mom?" Cassie asked, walking into the living room. "We're going to get some food from the cafeteria. I want you to meet Beth."

"Is Beth your employee?" her mom asked.

Cassie picked Petal up from her mom's lap and held her hand out to help her mom out of the sinking sofa. Petal jumped out of her arms and began another bath. "She's my friend, too."

They walked together down the gravel road to the cafeteria. It was break time for the campers.

"There she is," a girl yelled, and a group of girls ran toward them and blocked their path to the kitchen.

"Did you let the snake go?" one of the girls asked.

Melissa and her mother looked at each other.

"I sure did," Cassie answered. "It wasn't the kind of snake that would hurt anybody."

The girls screamed.

"Don't worry," Cassie said. "I released it a long way from here."

The girl with the braces had shiny pink lip gloss slathered across her mouth. "If you catch another one, will you show it to us?"

Cassie put her hands on her hips. "Well, that all depends."

The girls all blinked, waiting.

"Which one of you is going to help me catch it?" Cassie asked.

A couple of the girls shrieked, but two with linked arms held up their hands. When the girls had run over to the basketball courts, Melissa asked, "You have to catch snakes? There aren't snakes in your house, are there?"

When they walked into the kitchen, Beth was bent over a

cutting board, chopping carrots. She dropped her knife and met them inside the door.

"Beth, this is my mother, Nora, and my sister, Melissa."

Her mother reached out her hand to shake Beth's, but Beth shook her head. "Oh no you don't. I want a hug from Cassie's family."

Her mother's eyes widened as Beth wrapped her arms around her. Beth reached over to Melissa with her arms outstretched, but Melissa simply took her hands and gave her the same air kiss she had given Cassie.

"You must both be so proud of Cassie when you see the camp and everything she's responsible for," Beth said.

Cassie appreciated Beth's attempts. Cassie had to look down at the floor to keep them from seeing her smile at Beth's directed statement, but she did feel a little bad for her mom. Beth was making her squirm.

"Cassie works very hard," her mother said with a plastic smile plastered on her face.

Beth left to get lunch from the walk-in refrigerator. "She is. . ." Her mother stopped. "Very enthusiastic."

Cassie led them to a table at the edge of the dining room. "She's great. She keeps me sane."

Beth came out with three plates covered in cellophane—croissants with chicken salad and fresh strawberries. Cassie could tell she had taken extra time putting the sandwiches together and arranging the food on the plates.

As Cassie's mom and sister were devouring Beth's famous chicken salad and had forgotten their complaints about "cafeteria food," Beth motioned for Cassie to come into the kitchen. Cassie took a bite of her sandwich before excusing herself from the table.

Beth leaned against the edge of the sink. "Will called looking for you," she said in a grave tone.

Cassie's stomach tied itself in a knot. She looked out the door to make sure her mom and sister weren't listening. She didn't need them to know about Will and everything going on with the camp. She already felt inadequate enough. She didn't need the new failings in the relationship and career departments to confirm their opinions. "He knows I don't want to talk to him. Why doesn't he leave me alone?"

"He says he wants to explain and try to make things right."

Cassie wouldn't listen to his excuses. No amount of smooth talking or charm could get him out of this one. "Make what right? The fact that he wants to buy the camp and turn it into some kind of resort or that he wants to take our jobs and the camp from us? I don't want to talk to him."

Beth twisted her face. "So I'm guessing you forgot that he'll be here all weekend for the men's retreat."

Cassie groaned. The thought of Will spending three more days in her camp made her dizzy. Not to mention that her family would still be in town. "This is a disaster."

"He said he feels bad for keeping the meeting from you, but he didn't think you would understand."

Cassie's chest felt heavy. "He's right about that."

It was silent for a moment as Beth wrung her hands. "Cassie, he sounded pretty upset about you being mad at him."

She studied Beth's face. "If I didn't know better, I would think you're not as angry as I am."

"I'm pretty confused. I don't know what they talked about in that meeting, but he sounded so sincere on the phone."

"Beth?"

Her sister leaned back on the bench to see inside the kitchen. Cassie faked a smile. She took Beth's arm and pulled her farther into the kitchen. "Don't fall for that act. He said himself he gets away with a lot."

"Cassie," her mother called.

Beth gave her a sympathetic smile. Cassie sighed before walking into the dining room.

"Aren't you going to finish your sandwich?" her mom asked.

She sat beside her, but the thought of an entire weekend with Will Overman made her lose her appetite.

fourteen

A bell jingled as Cassie pushed open the store's glass door with TRASH TO TREASURE painted on it.

"Looks like they have more of the first than the latter," Melissa said inside the dark store.

Cassie's mom loved antique stores, and that was one thing Wyatt Bend had.

An old man sat behind a glass counter filled with baseball cards, costume jewelry, and toys Cassie remembered from her own childhood. He wore a flannel shirt with holes in the sleeve and a toboggan even though it was a hundred degrees outside.

The man turned the volume down on the sports talk blaring from his radio. "Are you ladies looking for anything in particular?"

"Just browsing," Cassie said, picking up a cookie jar shaped like a pig in overalls.

As they walked down a crowded aisle, Melissa stopped to inspect a pink dollhouse that looked older than her. "Mom has been looking for a music box."

Their mom stood across the room looking at a bookshelf full of paperback books.

"Really? Why a music box?"

Melissa wiped her hands together. "She lost one a long time ago that Grandpa Joe had given her. Every time she comes in a store like this she looks for one like it. It went missing when Dad left. I think he took it to be spiteful."

"I don't remember that story," Cassie said.

Melissa picked up a cup from its saucer. "Mom just told me a few years ago. There's a lot she didn't tell us back then. Trying to protect us, I guess."

Melissa knew so much about her mother that Cassie didn't. It had been Cassie's decision to move away from her family. Even though they could drive Cassie crazy, sometimes she questioned leaving.

Her mother picked up and opened every music box she passed but didn't purchase anything. Cassie noticed a basket of rose rocks beside the antique cash register.

"What are those?" Melissa asked.

"Rose rocks," the man said.

"They are sandy rocks that look like red roses. You can find them in this part of Oklahoma," Cassie explained. "I want to buy a couple for my nieces."

The man set a sandwich down on the paper plate beside him and wiped his hands on his jeans. "Are you ladies staying at the campground?"

He must have assumed they were tourists since he probably knew everyone who lived in the town. Another canyon near the camp was part of the state park and provided campgrounds and had RV hookups. It was a popular place for rock climbers and mountain biking.

Cassie's mom walked up behind them. "We're here to visit my daughter. She is the director of the church camp," she said, motioning to Cassie.

He pointed a finger toward Cassie's face. "You must be that girl dating Will Overman."

Cassie's face grew hot. "No, I'm not dating anyone."

The man laughed and slapped his hand against his knee. "Someone told me he keeps going down there to see you, and his daddy's not too happy about it."

Her mom cleared her throat. Cassie laid the money on the

counter. "I don't need a receipt, but thank you."

"I can't say I blame him for dating a pretty girl like you," he yelled out behind them.

Her mother walked quickly to the truck. By the time Cassie reached the door, her mother was already in her seat with her seat belt buckled and looking straight ahead. Cassie got in and shoved her key in the ignition.

"So. . . ," her mom said.

Cassie closed her eyes. "I am not dating anyone, Mom. I'm being honest."

Melissa grabbed the headrest on the front seat and leaned forward. "That guy seemed to think you were."

Cassie started the engine. "I understand you want to know, but I'm not dating anyone. And I really don't want to talk about it."

Her mother put a quarter lying on the floor of the truck in the cup holder. "Apparently he had some reason to believe you were dating this man. Do you know him?"

Cassie slid on a pair of old sunglasses she had stored in the console. "Yes," she said, giving up a little. "I know him. He was a counselor at the camp."

Her mom sucked in a long breath. "The counselor who found you when you broke your toe? How romantic. He rescued you."

Cassie shuttered. She put her hand on the back of the passenger seat and backed out of the parking place without answering.

"It was, wasn't it?" Melissa asked.

Cassie gave Melissa a look pleading for her not to encourage their mother. Melissa leaned back in her seat with a satisfied smirk.

"We never went out on a date, and I don't speak to him anymore, so it's a nonissue. I don't even know why we're talking about it."

"Why is the man at Trash to Treasure talking about it?"

"Because it's a small town, and people like to talk," Cassie said.

"Why aren't you speaking to him?" Melissa's question sounded more like a prompt for her mother.

Melissa's phone buzzed inside her purse, and she dug to find it. "Hello, honey. No, you can't feed her peaches. She breaks out in hives."

Her mother smoothed her hair with her hand. "I know you don't want to talk about this, but why don't you tell me what happened. Why would his father be unhappy that he sees you?"

Cassie pressed her lips together and looked back at Melissa who was rolling her eyes about something her husband had said.

"He didn't turn out to be who I thought he was," Cassie said.

"What do you mean?"

Cassie was silent for a moment. She wasn't used to talking about things like this with her mom.

"Well?" her mother persisted.

Cassie swallowed. "I think he was using me. I think it was all an act."

Her mother shook her head. "I see. I'm sorry to hear that."

Cassie realized that she and her mom had finally found something they had in common—falling for the wrong man.

❧

On Thursday morning Cassie had already been working for a couple of hours when Beth came in to start breakfast. Juggling between spending time with her family and scrambling to finish all her work at the camp hadn't been easy.

The next day would be tough. She and her staff would only have a few hours to turn over the camp between the end of the kids' camp and the start of the men's retreat. Not to mention she would be forced to face Will.

"I think this is the definition of burning the candle at both ends," Beth said.

Cassie didn't stop typing on her computer. "I know, but there is stuff I have to get finished no matter who is here."

Cassie handed Beth a pile of mail she hadn't had time to open, and without a word Beth began opening bills and sorting out the junk. "Are you nervous about seeing Will tomorrow?"

Cassie dreaded the awkwardness seeing him would bring and planned to lay low all weekend. "A little, but I'm determined to be perfectly professional."

"Have you thought about what it will be like to see him again?"

If only she could say she hadn't thought about Will, but it would have been a lie. She had thought about Will a lot. His face had popped into her head when she least expected it. "Hopefully he got the picture, and we won't have to talk about everything," Cassie said.

Beth tore a credit card application in half and set it in the pile of junk mail she had made on the desk. "He called again."

Cassie rolled her eyes. "When?"

"Yesterday when you were with Melissa and your mom. He said he's called your number several times, but you won't pick up or return his messages."

"They weren't messages about the retreat," Cassie said. "He just wants to talk about what happened, and I don't have anything to say to him."

Cassie could tell Beth was pretending to read the letter she had just opened. "What's wrong?"

Beth shrugged. "Nothing," she said, getting up from the chair. "I better get breakfast started."

"Wait a minute," Cassie said. "There's something you're not saying."

Beth sighed. "Listen. I'm just worried about you."

"Worried about me? What's there to be worried about?"

Beth picked up the junk mail from the desk and threw it in the trash. "You put up these walls. I'm just worried that you'll never think anyone is good enough for you."

Cassie pushed her chair back from the desk. "That's not true. Do you expect me to ignore everything that has happened with Will?"

"I was the first one to be suspicious of Will, and I'll admit he's made some pretty big mistakes," Beth said.

"But?"

Beth sighed. "But you're never going to find anybody if you expect them to be perfect."

Beth's words stung. "That's not fair. I don't expect anyone to be perfect."

"You won't even meet with Will to give him a chance to explain. I've never seen you as happy as you were when you were with Will. Maybe he's worth a chance."

Cassie breathed in a shaky breath: "Why are you taking up for him? He met with Mr. Hartley. Why can't you just be on my side?"

"I'm always on your side, Cassie. But not every man is your dad. You just have to give him a chance."

Cassie would have expected this from her mom or Melissa but not Beth.

"Just think about it, Cassie. I need to get breakfast started."

fifteen

The sight of Cassie walking across the lawn, her arms loaded with papers and folders, sent a charge of anxiety through Will. He was thankful for the chance to be near her this weekend. He was also unsure if the time together would bring them closer or confirm that they could never work past the issues that pulled them apart.

Will's father was ready to close the deal on Sunset Camp with Marvin Hartley. Will had petitioned him for more time, but time was running out. Will's desire to help the camp also hadn't gained him any points with his father when it came to trusting Will with bigger contracts.

If Cassie wasn't interested in Will's help, there wasn't much reason not to pursue the deal. If the camp was closing and they didn't purchase it, someone else would. But the idea of hurting Cassie haunted him.

Will left the group of guys who were checking in outside the meeting room doors and jogged across the grass to Cassie. He resisted the urge to brush the hair out of her eyes. "Can I help you with that?"

"Hi, Will," she said, her face barely moving. "I've got it, but thank you." She readjusted her arms around the load.

All business, as usual. Not exactly what he was hoping for. But what could he expect? "I thought you would try to avoid me this weekend, but here you are."

Cassie didn't react. "I was just on my way back to my office and wanted to make sure everything is running smoothly."

He would rather see her angry than for her to have no

emotion with him. He wasn't going to get anywhere with her like this. He bobbed his head in an exaggerated nod trying to hide his disappointment. He held up his itinerary. "So far, so good."

"Good. Let me know if you need anything."

He looked down at the stack of folders and paper in her arms. "What is all of that?"

For the first time, her expression broke. He had asked the wrong thing.

Cassie pulled the stack closer to her chest. "I'm using this to prepare for an upcoming meeting with the conference board."

Will was aware of every breath she took and how she leaned away from him. "Cassie, I don't blame you for not returning my calls," he said, taking a risk by crossing the line she had clearly drawn between them.

Cassie avoided his gaze.

"But I wanted a chance to explain myself," he said.

"We really don't need to talk about this now."

Maybe it was too late for "I'm sorry," but he had to try. Not wanting to lose his chance, he said, "I'm really sorry things got so complicated between us. I've done some things that weren't fair to you."

She didn't respond, only stared right through him.

"If we had met under different circumstances, I'd like to think things might have worked out between us."

A breeze rustled the papers in her arms. "Let's just focus on surviving this weekend."

Will's jaw clenched. "If it's what you want, Cassie."

Several of the men from his church had gathered nearby.

Cassie looked at them and back to Will. "I have to get back to work now."

"Wait," he said, desperate to stop her from walking away.

"These guys want to hike this weekend, and the only time I've been up the canyon was with you leading me in the dark."

"The path is easy," Cassie said. "If you follow it, it will lead you straight to the top of the canyon."

"They don't want to hike up the same trail as the grade-school kids. They want a challenge. Do you think you could go with us?"

The group of men had moved closer. They pretended not to listen, but none of them spoke.

She might not want to help him, but he knew Cassie. She always put the people staying in her camp first. Will leaned in closer to her. "I'm sure the last thing you want to do is spend any more time with me than you have to, but I'm trying to make this a good weekend for the guys."

Cassie bit her lip.

He could see her considering it. "Please," he pleaded. "I'll probably lead them off a cliff or something."

Cassie shifted back and forth. "I don't know. I have a lot of work to do."

"If it's your toe, I'll totally understand."

"It's not my toe, I just. . ."

The men stared at them. Cassie looked from her office to the group. When she didn't say anything, he nodded, disappointed. "Sorry, guys. She just has too much work to do. We can take the trail instead."

The men groaned. Cassie's shoulders slumped. "I'll do it."

"Really?" Will asked.

"I'll meet all of you beside the tabernacle tomorrow," Cassie said.

Will wanted to grab her and hug her. "Thank you. I owe you one."

⛭

Will's footsteps echoed down the dark hallway to Cassie's

office. He knocked his knuckle against the door. "Cassie, are you in there?"

No answer. He tried the door handle, but it was locked. He needed to talk to Cassie about accommodating one more man who wanted to come down for the last two days of the retreat. It also served as another excuse to be near her.

A figure of a woman walked toward him, but with the light to her back, he couldn't see her face. As she neared, he saw a lady with a short, red bob. He studied her familiar face, trying to place her. "If you're here for Cassie, like me, it looks like we're out of luck."

The woman's lips formed a tight line. "I don't know where that girl disappears to. Dinner is almost ready at the house."

He finally recognized her from the photo on Cassie's desk. Hadn't Cassie said she didn't get along with her family? "You're Cassie's mom."

The woman grinned. "Why, yes I am."

Will held his hand out to her. "I'm Will."

Her thin hand shook his. "I'm Nora. How did you know who I am?"

Will pointed a thumb at the door. "Cassie has a photo of you in her office."

She leaned back and put a hand on her heart. "She does?"

Will nodded. "Yes, ma'am."

Nora and Will ambled together down the hallway toward the door leading outside. "So, you're here all the way from Albuquerque?"

"Yes. Her sister and I came for a visit. How do you know Cassie?"

He held the door open for Nora and stepped out behind her into the still evening air. The setting sun had turned the sky hues of pink and blue. "We met when I volunteered as a counselor here. This weekend I'm here as part of a men's retreat."

A glint in her eye told him she was like his mother and didn't miss much when it came to her kids. "You wouldn't happen to be the gentleman who helped my daughter when she hurt her toe, would you?"

The idea that Cassie had talked about him to her mother excited him, but Nora might know more than he would have hoped. "That would be me."

She raised an eyebrow at him. "I see."

He gave her a sideways glance. "How much do you know about me?"

"Unfortunately, she doesn't tell me as much as I would like. My daughter has trouble opening up to people. Even her mother."

Will knew about that all too well. "Where are you headed?"

"Back to Cassie's house. Would you like to walk with me?"

Will glanced at the men playing basketball on the courts. "I would love to."

"Cassie's a wonderful girl," Nora said. "So headstrong and independent."

"I agree wholeheartedly."

She smiled at him. "I figured you would."

Will looked down at Nora. She was petite, just like Cassie. "She can also be a tough one to figure out."

Nora nodded. "She had some rough times when she was a kid, and that's given her some extra hurdles, especially when dealing with men."

Will didn't want to press her too hard, but he was interested at the chance to get a glimpse into Cassie's heart. "Like what?"

They strolled onto the gravel drive that ran through the camp. "Unlike my youngest daughter, Cassie was a daddy's girl from the day she was born. After her father left us when Cassie was ten, he would call her and tell her he was coming back home or that he was sending her a plane ticket to come visit him. She would get so excited and tell all of her friends. He let her down every single time," Nora said, her voice cracking.

Will's protective impulses coursed through him. How could someone do that to his own daughter?

"This went on for years. Eventually she created this hard little shell around her that I still haven't figured out how to break through."

Will's chest ached for Cassie. After being let down so many times before, finding out about his meeting with Mr. Hartley must have felt all too familiar to her. No wonder she had reacted like she did.

"It breaks my heart that the problems between her father and I are still affecting her," Nora said. "I'm afraid she'll never trust anyone."

Will stared down at his feet as he walked. "I've been an idiot."

Nora stopped. "What are you talking about?"

Will shook his head. "I think she started to trust me, and I destroyed it. I just wish she would give me a chance to try to fix it. Any advice for me?"

Nora pointed at his chest. "You need to be patient with her. She's worth the wait. If it's right, it will happen."

"I hope you're right, Nora."

☙

On Saturday the group of guys thanked Cassie as they followed her through the trees to the path up the canyon. They quickly moved off the trail to a steeper slope covered with rocks and roots obstructing their route. She led them toward the most challenging means to the top of the canyon wall that didn't include rock climbing. Will stayed at the front of the pack of hikers near Cassie but turned around every few minutes to stop and encourage the men or tease the guys about their progress. "We better not tell Elizabeth about this," he said to a man in his early twenties. "Your honey-do list will get even longer if she knows you have this much energy."

It was obvious by the way the men laughed and bantered back that they respected him.

"I think Gary is part mountain lion," he said to a balding man scrambling up a stone.

If only this was the sole side of Will, but she had already seen him as the sneaky and self-interested businessman. To trust him now would be naive.

By the time they reached the top, most of the men's shirts dripped with sweat and were stained with orange from the rocks they climbed. Cassie moved to the back of the pack and let them enjoy their reward—the view from the summit.

Not even out of breath, Will looked like he had taken an elevator to the top. He came and stood by Cassie, his hands buried deep in his pockets.

"Does everything come so easily to you?" The words slipped out of her mouth too easily.

Will leaned forward and looked in her eyes. "Is that what you think of me? That I've had everything handed to me?"

She had offended him. She wasn't trying to be hurtful. There was so much she wanted to say to him, but she couldn't find the right words. "I'm not talking about your family. I'm talking about you. When people look at you, they see someone who has it all together. Someone who knows exactly what he's doing."

Will's gaze went over her head. "Cassie, there's more to me than what you see."

There was a silence between them that Cassie didn't know how to break. The conversation hadn't gone where she had meant for it to go. She didn't know how to get everything back where it needed to be.

Will cleared his throat. "Cassie, is there any chance for us to put this behind us? To try to separate the business from us?"

If only it could be that easy. Cassie checked to see if the men were listening, but they were all looking out over the edge of the canyon or sitting on boulders resting before their trek down the trail. She pursed her lips together. "I don't think you understand how much I love this camp."

Will opened and closed his hand at his side. "That's just it, Cassie. I love it here, too. I wanted to explain that to you."

Cassie faced him. "Then why did you sneak behind my back? Why did you meet with Mr. Hartley?"

Will held open hands out to her. "I'm sorry for not telling you."

"But you're not sorry for the meeting or for trying to buy the camp."

"I know it looks bad, but you have it all wrong."

Cassie didn't trust him. She couldn't.

"We talked to him about buying the camp if it was going under," Will said. "But I also talked to him about ways to help you save the camp."

Cassie wanted to believe he had good intentions, but telling her he was helping her by meeting with her boss was ludicrous. "Helping me would be to stay out of it. Now that Mr. Hartley knows someone is interested in this place, my chances of saving it have gone down the tubes."

Will looked up toward the sky. "I'll be honest, Mr. Hartley isn't sold on the idea of working to save this place, but you have to believe me, I've been doing everything I can to convince him."

"And if you don't convince him?" Cassie asked. "What happens then?"

Will rubbed his hand across the back of his neck. "My father wants to pursue purchasing the camp, but if it's closing anyway. . ."

Resentment coursed through her. "Okay, Will. Here's your chance." She stepped away from him. "If your intentions with Mr. Hartley were good, tell me why you kept it a secret. All that time we spent together, you never thought it might be something I should know."

Will's fists clinched. "I don't know," he murmured. "I guess I thought I was trying to protect you."

Cassie bit the inside of her cheek. "I don't need you to protect me, Will. I really don't." She turned to leave, but he cupped his hand on her elbow. She stopped.

"Cassie, please look at me."

She spun around and crossed her arms on her chest.

The shadows under his eyes made him appear worn down. "I need you to trust me."

"Will, I—"

"No, Cassie. Please listen to what I have to say." He reached out to her but withdrew his hand before he touched her. "I know asking you to trust me on this is a lot to ask. I know it won't be easy. But give me another chance."

"I've given you enough chances." Without missing a beat, she whistled. "Hey, guys. Let's head back down to camp."

As the group gathered around her, Will stood stone-faced. When she looked behind her, Will sat on a boulder with his head in his hands.

sixteen

That night Cassie stood at her kitchen sink, filling a pot with water. Her mom walked in behind her. "I think I'm all packed to leave in the morning."

"I can't believe you're leaving already," Cassie said.

Her mom and sister going home was bittersweet for Cassie. They still drove her crazy at times, but she never could have imagined she would be so sad to see them go.

Her mom took the pot of water from Cassie's hands and set it on the stove. "I took a walk this evening. The canyon was absolutely beautiful."

Cassie was happy her mom was finally beginning to see what she saw in the camp. If only the camp's survival wasn't at stake. "That's great, Mom."

Her mother turned the burner on high. "I met Will Overman while I was down there," she said nonchalantly.

Cassie's shoulders tensed at the mention of his name. Will had a knack for secret meetings with the important people in Cassie's life. "You did?"

Her mom poured salt into her palm and then dusted it into the pot. "He seems like a nice young man."

Cassie pulled a skillet from a cabinet beside the stove. "Sure. He seems nice." Unfortunately, there were two sides to Will.

"He's obviously torn up about whatever happened between you two," her mother said.

Cassie should have known he would try to charm her

mom, too. She placed her hands on her hips. "Why? What did he say?"

"That he had been an idiot."

Cassie dropped her arms and opened the refrigerator door. "Well, at least he knows it."

"Cassie." Her mother's voice softened. "I know I butt into your business more than I should and that you don't necessarily want to hear your old mom's advice."

Cassie took a green pepper from the drawer and closed the refrigerator door. "Go ahead, Mom. What do you have to say?"

Her mother didn't answer at first. "I think you should give him another chance."

First Beth, now her mom. Just because Cassie acted strong didn't mean she could deal with a broken heart. She shook her head. "You don't understand, Mom. It's impossible."

Her mother hugged her and whispered, "Nothing's impossible, darling."

Cassie blinked back the tears in her eyes. "This is. It's too messy."

Her mom held Cassie's elbows and forced her to look into her eyes. "Listen to me. I don't want you to ever hide from something wonderful because of fear or because of the mistakes I made."

Melissa walked in from the living room. "What are you two talking about? It's so serious in here."

Still surprised by what her mom had said, Cassie watched her as she ignored Melissa and pulled a cutting board from the cabinet. Until then, Cassie hadn't realized her mom felt responsible for Cassie being alone.

After her mom and sister had gone to bed, Cassie sat in a rocking chair on her back porch. She couldn't hear any cars from her house, and there weren't any airports nearby. The camp below was quiet. All she could hear was the breeze rustling the leaves and the crickets chirping.

She stared out into the trees behind her house and pulled the quilt more tightly around her shoulders. She had to remind herself the Will in the camp right now wasn't the Will who had spent an evening star watching with her or the one who sent her flowers. That wasn't the real Will. It couldn't be. That Will wouldn't have gone behind her back to hurt her and the camp for a business deal.

Lord, where do I go from here?

The back door slid open, and Cassie jumped in her seat.

Melissa wore pink satin pajamas, a satin robe, and matching slippers. She looked beautiful, even in the middle of the night, and Cassie felt underdressed in her flannel pants and T-shirt. "What are you doing out here? It's two in the morning."

"Sometimes I have trouble sleeping," Cassie said. "You?"

"Thirsty, and I saw you were out here."

Melissa went back into the kitchen and came back with a glass of water and a dish towel she laid in the dusty seat before sitting. They sat in silence for a moment.

"Do you miss your girls and Daniel when you're away from home?" Cassie asked.

Melissa grinned. "I miss them so much. Don't get me wrong—it has been great to have a break, but I don't feel like myself when I'm away from them." Melissa turned to her. "Do you ever think about getting married and having kids?"

"Of course. I would love that."

"Really?"

Cassie looked up at the sky. It was clear, and the stars were shining. "It's not like Mom makes it out to be. I can't put a billboard up for a husband. And I'm okay with being single."

"But you also can't close yourself off to the possibility. You have to put yourself in situations to meet someone."

Melissa and Daniel had met in high school. "I've just always assumed that when it's meant to be, God will make it happen," Cassie said.

Melissa took a long drink. "Does it get lonely out here by yourself?"

Cassie didn't know what she meant. Lonely in Oklahoma without family? Without a man in her life? With a house in the quiet canyon? "I don't really think about it like that. I have Beth and the rest of the staff, my friends from church, and lots of rowdy kids in the camp. I don't have much time to think about being lonely," she said. Or maybe she didn't let herself have time to be lonely.

It had been different since Will had been around. Then everything had gotten turned upside down.

Melissa crossed her arms at her waist. "Sometimes I think about how lucky you are."

Lucky? Cassie turned to look at her sister.

"Don't look so surprised," Melissa said. "You got to have a career and make close friends who aren't your friends because your husbands all work at the same place. You can move, figure out what you love to do."

"I thought you loved being a mom. You're so good at it."

Melissa tucked her hair behind both ears. "Oh, I do love being a mom, more than anything else in the world," she said quickly. "But sometimes there is so much pressure from other people."

Cassie had never heard her sister talk this openly about her own struggles. It was always about how great her life was.

"We constantly have to keep up with whatever his coworkers are doing—house, car, private school. His mom doesn't think much of me. She thinks I purposefully don't bring the kids over enough, but she doesn't realize it's hard work getting the kids loaded up and driving them by myself for three hours for such a short visit." Her sister appeared so vulnerable.

"I didn't know," Cassie said.

"And then there is Mom," her sister said. "She's always asking me if I plan to finish college, which I tell her of course I would love to do, but it's not the easiest thing to find the time and money with two kids."

Cassie didn't know her mom saw Melissa as anything but perfect. She squeezed her sister's arm. "You know I'm really proud of you."

Melissa laughed.

"No, I'm serious. My baby sister has it all. She has a great husband and two girls, and she has done an amazing job raising them."

Melissa bit her bottom lip. "Thank you. It means a lot."

"I get so caught up with everything here, and sometimes I forget to tell you. I'm sorry for that."

Melissa smiled with her lips pressed together. "Mom told me about Will. Do you want to talk about it?"

Cassie didn't have the energy to be angry at her mom for telling Melissa. They talked every day, and keeping secrets wasn't her mom's strong point. She cringed when she thought about how much her mom might have told Will during their talk. "I don't know."

An owl cried in the tree above her.

"I'm sorry it didn't work out with him," Melissa said.

Cassie felt an ache deep in her chest. She pulled her knees up against her body and leaned back in the chair. "I don't know anything about him. I can't believe anything he's ever told me. The hardest part is he's still the guy I fell for, but at the same time, he's not."

Melissa took a long drink of water. "Love is hard. Daniel and I still have to work to keep ours strong."

"Really?"

Melissa shrugged. "It's tough to have your heart in someone else's hands."

A lump formed in Cassie's throat. "How do you know they won't trample on it?"

Melissa shook her head. "You don't."

Cassie stared out into the darkness. "Then what makes love worth the risk?"

Melissa leaned on the arm of the chair, and a shadow covered her face. "You still care about him, don't you?"

"What makes you say that?"

"Because I've never seen my big sister actually calculating the cost."

Cassie shook her head. "It's too late for us. At this point I don't even know how to fix it."

"Sure you do," Melissa said.

She looked at her sister. "I do?"

Melissa opened her eyes wide. "Of course. Deep down you know."

Cassie had been thinking about Will from the moment he walked into her camp, and she still hadn't figured him out. How could she know?

Melissa leaned forward in her chair. "But usually whatever it is just seems too big or too difficult or too scary."

Cassie's pulse raced.

Melissa smiled. "If you love him, really love him, you'll figure out how to do that big, scary thing."

Cassie felt like God had been chiseling away at all the

darkest places of her heart during the past few weeks, and it had been difficult and painful. Right now she felt like He had cracked her heart wide open, and she knew what she had to do.

seventeen

Will and his father walked out of the small room they used as their conference room. "Do you think you could get those estimates finished by the end of the week?" Will's father asked.

Since returning from the retreat, Will operated on autopilot. His attempts to make things right with Cassie had failed, and he came back to an office full of work to close the deal on Sunset Camp. "I'll take care of it," he told his father.

"Will." His sister smiled at him from the receptionist's desk. She motioned her head toward the door. "Cassie is here to see you."

The air rushed out of him.

Cassie stood at the front of the office, her hands hanging loose at her sides. "Hi, Will."

Hope sprung up in his chest, but he pushed it away. Cassie despised him. He had hurt her, and he was paying the price. What was she doing here?

His father stepped between them. "Are you going to introduce us?"

"Sure. I'm sorry," Will said, floundering for the right words to say. "This is Cassie Langley, director of Sunset Camp."

His father reached a hand out to her.

"Cassie, this is my father, Leonard Overman."

She looked pretty in jeans and a light blue top. Her face was pale, and she appeared more nervous than he had ever seen her. "It's a pleasure to meet you."

Will's father clapped his hands together. "Well, what can we do for you, young lady?"

Please don't scare her away, Dad.

She swallowed and stared at Will. "Um. Well, actually, I came to ask Will if his offer still stood." Her voice shook.

"Offer?" his father said. "What offer would that be?"

Will waited for her answer.

Cassie took a deep breath. "As you know, the camp is still in some financial trouble, and Will had kindly offered to help me work through some of those issues. Now I see how beneficial that could be for the camp, and I've rethought my refusal."

Will's heartbeat pounded in his chest. Cassie was here with her guard down asking for him to come alongside her and save Sunset Camp.

His dad shook his head. "I'm sorry, but it's not quite that simple. We—"

Will walked toward Cassie. "Dad, let her finish."

Cassie stood up straighter. "I know you've been working with Mr. Hartley to purchase the property, but if you consider the purpose of the camp and the good we could do there, you might reconsider." Before giving them time to respond, Cassie said, "I respect that this is something you'll need to talk about. I appreciate your time. Will knows where to reach me."

Cassie spun around and was out the door. Will followed her and caught her as she opened the door to her truck. "Wow. What just happened in there?"

Her big brown eyes stared up at him. "I know it's probably too late, but I've been pushing you away because I was afraid. It wasn't fair to you or the camp."

He nodded, understanding how hard this was for her. "I'll need to work out a lot of things with my family and Mr.

Hartley. It's not going to be easy."

Cassie nodded. "The board meeting is on Saturday, so there isn't much time," she said.

A hundred questions ran through Will's mind. Was it too late? Would his dad and brother agree to it? Could he get Marvin Hartley to agree to it? Would Cassie get scared and change her mind again?

Cassie, the woman who lived her life wearing a suit of armor, had come to him and dropped her defenses. If she saw that she could trust him with this, maybe she would be able to trust him with her heart.

eighteen

The next few days were a whirlwind for Cassie. Not only did she have a canyon full of campers, but she felt like she had left her heart with Will. With each day that passed without hearing from him, the more difficult it was to stay hopeful.

No matter what happened with Will, she would do everything she could to make a case for the camp to the board.

On Saturday morning the camp was eerily quiet, and today the silence haunted her. Beth had offered to help her set up for the board meeting, but Cassie had given her the day off. Mr. Hartley's town car pulled into the canyon exactly an hour before the meeting was scheduled to begin. Cassie's palms were damp and her eye twitched—not the first impression she wanted to make on the board.

As the car approached, she saw Mr. Hartley was alone. His tie was tied tightly under a shirt collar that was turned up at the ends and badly in need of a pressing.

After he parked he opened the trunk and pulled out a large box.

"Can I help you with anything?" she asked as he approached.

He hoisted it up in his arms. "No, I'm fine. Which room have you set up for our meeting?"

She led him to the largest small-group area. Three long tables were set up in a U shape. In front of each chair, Cassie had placed a booklet of papers complete with financial information, bios on the staff at the camp, a list of campers, and even copies of touching letters she had received from campers.

He handed her a stack of papers to be laid out at each chair. "We'll need three more chairs. The Overmans will be in attendance."

She nodded, but inside she felt nauseous. Will not telling her he would be there and having his family with him were both signs of bad news. Her legs wobbled as she carried three more chairs into the room and made copies of her presentation.

Once everything was ready, she sat in one of the seats and waited, but eventually her nerves kicked into high gear. She needed to escape the walls that seemed to be closing in on her. She headed across the camp to the chapel. The air inside was warm and still, and light poured in through the stained-glass windows.

She rubbed her hands together trying to work out the nerves. She broke a spiderweb from the wall with the tip of her finger and walked to the small wooden railing. She placed her knees on the red velvet cushion on the bottom and leaned her body weight onto her elbows on the wooden rail.

Everything she carried with her was too heavy to bear. She had prayed so hard for God to save the camp. She had even listened to Him when He led her to accept Will's help. Had God abandoned her, too? She had been let down so many times—by her father, by Will. Her soul felt clenched like white knuckles on the steering wheel, driving through the pouring rain. She had been holding on so tightly for so long, she wasn't sure she knew how to let go.

"Do not be afraid or terrified because of them, for the Lord your God goes with you; he will never leave you nor forsake you."

She remembered the verse from the day she asked Mr.

Hartley to give her a chance to fight for the camp. A tear fell on her folded hands, and she realized they were streaming down her cheeks. She couldn't do it anymore, not alone. She needed God's help. It wasn't in her hands, and she accepted that.

The heaviness lifted off her chest and head. God didn't tell her He would save the camp or if she would still have her job, but He was going to take care of her. Her heart overflowed with faith that He was in control.

When she returned to the meeting room, the board members were filing through the door. Will Overman stood in the room with his back to Cassie. He wore a gray suit and worked setting up an easel and a presentation board covered in charts and figures. His brother sat at the table and flipped through the reports in front of him, and Will's father stood in the corner of the room, talking to one of the board members.

When Will turned and looked at her, Cassie felt hollow.

Mr. Hartley stood in front of the group before Will had an opportunity to speak to her. He appeared even more nervous and flustered than usual. "Because we have guests in our meeting today who would like to be a part of the discussion about the issues we are facing with this particular camp, I would like to begin with that item on the agenda."

Cassie couldn't bear to look at Will.

Mr. Hartley held up one of the stapled stacks of paper he had brought with him. "You should all be familiar with the financial outlook of the camp because we've gone over it during the last two meetings. You should all have a copy in front of you for your review."

The room filled with the sound of pages flipping. Mr. Hartley led them through all the details of the camp, realities Cassie lived with every day. According to the numbers they looked at, it would be a better financial decision to close Sunset Camp and integrate all the camps held there into the nearest camp in another part of the state.

Mr. Hartley pointed at Cassie. "Miss Langley, who is serving as the interim director, would like to say a few words and present some information about the camp to us before we vote. If you have any questions, I'm sure she would also be happy to entertain those as well."

He nodded to Cassie who stood and walked on shaky legs to the front of the long table.

Will's eyes were on her, but Cassie avoided his gaze. Instead she made eye contact with the board members waiting for her to speak.

"Honestly," she said, trying to hide the tremble in her voice, "I may not be the most objective person to look at whether or not the camp should stay open. This isn't because I would lose my job, but because God used this camp to change my life when I was a camper, and I have seen Him change countless other lives here."

Will leaned forward in his chair.

"So I believe I have a lot of vital information for you on where the money is and where the camp is going that could help you see why this camp should survive. But in all actuality, I believe this camp should be here because God does some great work down here in this canyon. I understand that this is a business decision, and I respect that. Please also consider the impact this camp has on the hearts of everyone who comes here."

The board members stared at her without expression on their faces. Cassie led the group through the factors and numbers that Mr. Hartley didn't present, including the reasons the outgo appeared larger this year because of all the old debts and bills the former director had failed to pay. "Finally, I'd like to say thank you for giving me the opportunity to speak here today. If you take one thing away from what I've said, please know that if you give this camp more time, we can turn it around. Think of the history and the effect it has had on the lives of so many. It deserves another chance."

When she sat, no one said a word; they only stared at her.

"Are there any questions or comments?" Mr. Hartley asked from his seat.

"I was a camper here," a woman in a suit jacket said. She looked out the window wistfully. She pointed toward the canyon wall. "I was right over there when I became a Christian during a small-group meeting."

Another board member leaned over and patted her arm.

After the room was silent for a moment, Mr. Hartley said, "I think we should move on. We still need to give Mr. Overman the chance to speak."

Cassie's face and neck burned as she watched Will take the floor. She focused on breathing, hoping she could sit through what he had to say. Will straightened his tie as he walked by Cassie.

"I would like to begin by thanking Mr. Hartley for allowing me, my father, Leonard, and my brother Connor to be here today. I think we've come up with some great plans for the camp if you decide to go in this direction, and after looking at the numbers, I think you'll agree."

Cassie held her breath and braced herself for everything to fall apart. He stared straight at Cassie as he spoke, but she broke his gaze.

"I'm pleased to say we're here to offer our time and our combined years of experience to make sure this camp survives. We've decided that it's important for the area to have a place like Sunset Camp, and I think we can help."

Cassie looked up at Will, her mouth open in disbelief. He nodded at her.

"I think there are some opportunities for additional income for the camp if we just take advantage of them. I've done some research on camps with similar facilities bringing in about half of their income by making the facilities available for renting and even catering from the cafeteria. With the facilities and talented staff already here, I think it could be a smooth transition, and we wouldn't have to sacrifice the original vision for the camp."

The board members nodded as he spoke. Will continued to explain all the ways he had mapped out for the camp to get back on its financial footing. Cassie struggled to hold back the tears.

When Will finished his presentation, Mr. Hartley asked them to leave the room so they could discuss the item and vote. Cassie, Will, Connor, and Leonard filed out of the room. Connor and Leonard flipped open their mobile phones and headed out in different directions.

When she and Will walked toward the grass, Cassie reached out and wrapped her arms around him, almost knocking him backward. "I don't know how I could ever thank you for what you've done."

He hugged her back. "This is enough."

She pulled back to see his face. "I mean it. I turned you away so many times. I couldn't have blamed you if you hadn't bothered to help me."

His eyes were warm, and his face relaxed. "I'm really sorry I didn't tell you I would be here."

She smiled at him. It was impossible for her to be irritated after what he had done for her. "Why didn't you?"

Will shook his head. "There was no time. I didn't want to say anything until I was absolutely sure, and it took every minute I had to convince Mr. Hartley and my father that it was the right thing to do."

Cassie looked to the window of the meeting room. The faces at the table all turned up to Mr. Hartley. "What made Mr. Hartley change his mind?"

"Well, Hartley had a hard time with the concept of a developer working with one of his camp directors."

"Why?" Cassie asked.

"According to him, Henry Mason was letting the camp crash because another developer agreed to cut him in on the deal."

Cassie shook her head in disbelief, but it explained all the incorrect books and the unpaid debts. "I can't believe he would do that."

"It made Mr. Hartley extra cautious about us working together, and from what I hear around town, everyone thinks we have a relationship outside of camp business anyway."

They would have plenty to talk about now. Cassie laughed. "What about your dad?"

Will stared out toward the nurse's cabin where Will's father stood on the porch on the phone. "It took him a few days, but he came around. It's not hard to see how many lives this place has changed."

Cassie thought about how much his family must have given up for Will to do what he did.

"Plus, I told him how I feel about you. You wouldn't ever guess it, but he's a romantic at heart. Just ask my mom."

A charge of electricity raced through Cassie. "So what did you tell him about us?"

Will stepped closer to her. "That if you ever gave me another chance, I would be a fool to mess it up. That you were the kind of girl I've been searching for."

She reached for his hand and intertwined his fingers with hers.

Will motioned at the meeting room with his head. "Are you nervous about what's going on in there?"

Cassie shook her head. "It's in God's hands now."

epilogue

Cassie sat straight up in bed and looked around, disoriented. Her eyes fought to adjust to the dark room. Then someone pounded on her front door.

She groaned as she climbed out from under the covers. She pulled her bathrobe off the hook on the door and slipped it around her. "Just a minute," she called.

She shuffled through the house, turning on lights on her way to the front door. Through the peephole, Beth stared back at her. She opened the door. "Come in. What's going on?"

Beth looked wide awake. "We have campers out of their cabins again. Up for a hike?"

Cassie groaned. "I guess there's not much choice."

"I've already told the counselors where they need to look," Beth said.

Cassie yawned. "Let me change."

Cassie and Beth walked silently toward the canyon wall. As they trudged through the darkness, she thought about Will. She couldn't wait to call him in the morning and tell him that she had hiked through the darkness looking for teenagers again.

Will and Cassie had been together for just over a year now, and it had been an amazing journey.

Mr. Hartley had offered Cassie the permanent director position after the meeting, and with Will's help, almost twice as many people had visited Sunset Camp this year than the last.

Weddings, family reunions, and corporate retreats had taken place in the canyon. The weddings had been held in the tabernacle, in the chapel, and outside under the trees. Beth had catered most of them and was beginning to be well known for her food. She had even made a few of the wedding cakes.

Most importantly, Cassie had fallen more in love with Will than she could have ever imagined.

Cassie and Beth turned on the trail leading up the canyon. When Beth nudged her and motioned toward the steep incline, Cassie nodded.

She followed behind Beth in the dark slowly, making sure her footing was solid as she pulled herself up with the rope.

When she reached the top, she took the hand that reached for hers. She flinched when the hand she held wasn't Beth's.

"It's okay. It's me."

Cassie's stomach fluttered. "Will? What are you doing out here in the middle of the night?"

The darkness gave way to a soft glow of light. Cassie looked over to a beaming Beth lighting votive candles lined up on a log.

Cassie's heart pounded so hard she was sure Will and Beth could hear it. "What's going on?" But when Cassie looked into Will's eyes, she knew. Cassie pressed her hand against her chest and took a deep breath. They weren't there to find campers. Will had planned out every detail of this for her.

Will dropped to one knee on the orange dirt. "Cassie Langley, I love you. I thank God every day for bringing you into my life. Your spirit and your strength are beautiful. I want nothing more than to spend the rest of my life with you."

Cassie clasped her hands over her mouth. Tears ran down her face.

Will pulled a little square box out of his pocket and opened it to reveal a ring that sparkled in the moonlight. "Will you marry me?"

Cassie nodded her head, no words coming out. She pulled him to his feet, and he wrapped his arms around her.

"Yes," she whispered in his ear. "A million times, yes."

A Letter To Our Readers

Dear Reader:

In order that we might better contribute to your reading enjoyment, we would appreciate your taking a few minutes to respond to the following questions. We welcome your comments and read each form and letter we receive. When completed, please return to the following:

Fiction Editor
Heartsong Presents
PO Box 719
Uhrichsville, Ohio 44683

1. Did you enjoy reading *Canyon Walls* by Julie Jarnagin?
   ❏ Very much! I would like to see more books by this author!
   ❏ Moderately. I would have enjoyed it more if

   _____

   _____

   _____

2. Are you a member of **Heartsong Presents**? ❏ Yes ❏ No
   If no, where did you purchase this book? _____

   _____

3. How would you rate, on a scale from 1 (poor) to 5 (superior), the cover design? _____

4. On a scale from 1 (poor) to 10 (superior), please rate the following elements.

   ____ Heroine   ____ Plot
   ____ Hero   ____ Inspirational theme
   ____ Setting   ____ Secondary characters

5. These characters were special because? _____

_____

_____

6. How has this book inspired your life? _____

_____

_____

7. What settings would you like to see covered in future
   Heartsong Presents books? _____

_____

_____

8. What are some inspirational themes you would like to see
   treated in future books? _____

_____

_____

9. Would you be interested in reading other **Heartsong
   Presents** titles?   ❏ Yes   ❏ No

10.   Please check your age range:

   ❏ Under 18   ❏ 18-24
   ❏ 25-34   ❏ 35-45
   ❏ 46-55   ❏ Over 55

Name _____

Occupation _____

Address _____

City, State, Zip _____

E-mail _____

OREGON WEDDINGS

3 stories in 1

Love reigns in the Pacific
Northwest as three
wounded hearts allow
romance and faith to heal
past hurts and overcome
present fears.

Contemporary, paperback, 352 pages, 5.1875" x 8"

Please send me _____ copies of *Black Hills Blessing*. I am enclosing $7.99 for each.
(Please add $4.00 to cover postage and handling per order. OH add 7% tax.
If outside the U.S. please call 740-922-7280 for shipping charges.)

Name _____

Address _____

City, State, Zip _____

Heart♥ng

HEARTSONG PRESENTS TITLES AVAILABLE NOW:

___HP729 *Bay Hideaway*, B. Loughner
___HP730 *With Open Arms*, J. L. Barton
___HP754 *Red Like Crimson*, J. Thompson
___HP758 *Wedded Bliss*, K. Y'Barbo
___HP762 *Photo Op*, L. A. Coleman
___HP785 *If the Dress Fits*, D. Mayne
___HP786 *White as Snow*, J. Thompson
___HP789 *The Bride Wore Coveralls*, D. Ullrick
___HP790 *Garlic and Roses*, G. Martin
___HP806 *Out of the Blue*, J. Thompson
___HP814 *The Preacher Wore a Gun*, J. Livingston
___HP817 *By the Beckoning Sea*, C. G. Page
___HP818 *Buffalo Gal*, M. Connealy
___HP821 *Clueless Cowboy*, M. Connealy
___HP830 *The Bossy Bridegroom*, M. Connealy
___HP834 *Salt Water Taffie*, J. Hanna
___HP838 *For the Love of Books*, D. R. Robinson
___HP850 *Trail to Justice*, S. P. Davis
___HP865 *Always Ready*, S. P. Davis
___HP885 *A Hero for Her Heart*, C. Speare & N. Toback
___HP886 *Romance by the Book*, M. Johnson
___HP889 *Special Mission*, D. Mayne
___HP890 *Love's Winding Path*, L. Bliss
___HP893 *Disarming Andi*, E. Goddard
___HP894 *Crossroads Bay*, K. Kovach
___HP897 *Polar Opposites*, S. P. Davis
___HP898 *Parting Secrets*, B. Melby & C. Wienke

___HP901 *Gaining Love*, J. Johnson
___HP902 *White Roses*, S. T. Vannattes
___HP905 *Boxed into Love*, C. Speare & N. Toback
___HP906 *Perfect Ways*, J. Odell
___HP909 *Portrait of Love* , D. Mayne
___HP910 *Where the Dogwoods Bloom*, M. Johnson
___HP913 *Exposing Amber* , G. Goddard
___HP914 *Heart of Mine* , L. Bliss
___HP917 *Pure Serendipity*, B. Melby & C. Wienke
___HP918 *Fine, Feathered Friend*, K. Kovach
___HP921 *White Doves*, S. T. Vannatter
___HP922 *Maid to Love*, J. Johnson
___HP925 *Mending Fences*, C. Speare & N. Toback
___HP926 *The Thing about Beauty*, D. Robinson
___HP929 *Facing Tessa's Past*, M. Colvin
___HP930 *Wasatch Love*, L. Bliss
___HP933 *Praying for Rayne*, E. Goddard
___HP934 *Lily of the Field*, R. R. Zediker
___HP937 *White Pearls*, S. T. Vannatter
___HP938 *Betting on Love*, J. Johnson
___HP941 *In the Cool of the Evening*, J. Spaeth
___HP942 *Peace, Be Still*, T. Fowler
___HP945 *Perfect Peace*, J. Odell
___HP946 *Redeeming Sarah's Present*, M. Colvin

(If ordering from this page, please remember to include it with the order form.)

Presents

Great Inspirational Romance
at a Great Price!

Heartsong Presents books are inspirational romances in contemporary and historical settings, designed to give you an enjoyable, spirit-lifting reading experience. You can choose wonderfully written titles from some of today's best authors like Wanda E. Brunstetter, Mary Connealy, Susan Page Davis, Cathy Marie Hake, Joyce Livingston, and many others.

When ordering quantities less than six, above titles are $3.99 each.
Not all titles may be available at time of order.